Suddenly, Reese could see Corinne by his side, on his arm, in his home, in his . . .

Reese paced the floor. Corinne had no place in his life, certainly not that of a wife, and she never would. She was engaged to marry another man, and that man was not only a neighbor and a friend of sorts, but he was an employee and a good one. Whatever Reese's interest in Corinne Terral was, the woman was taken. Period. No discussion needed. He was attracted to her, but that didn't mean he could or should court her.

Court her? Reese was beginning to wish he'd never laid eyes on her. Certainly he regretted having agreed to this role of caretaker. But how was he to know that she'd be so lovely? How could he ever have predicted this attraction? Well, he wouldn't let this be a problem. Corinne Terral was a lovely, compelling woman, but she was someone else's lovely, compelling woman, and Reese wasn't about to forget that, not for a moment. Not for a single moment . . .

Dear Reader,

Welcome to Silhouette Romance—experience the magic of the wonderful world where two people fall in love. Meet heroines who will make you cheer for their happiness, and heroes (be they the boy next door or a handsome, mysterious stranger) who will win your heart. Silhouette Romance reflects the magic of love—sweeping you away with books that will make you laugh and cry; heartwarming, poignant stories that will move you time and time again.

In the next few months, we're publishing romances by many of your all-time favorites such as Diana Palmer, Brittany Young, Annette Broadrick and many others. Your response to these authors and others in Silhouette Romance has served as a touchstone for us, and we're pleased to bring you more books with Silhouette's distinctive medley of charm, wit and—above all—*romance*.

During 1991, we have many special events planned. Don't miss our WRITTEN IN THE STARS series. Each month in 1991, we're proud to present you with a book that focuses on the hero—and his astrological sign.

I hope you'll enjoy this book and all of the stories to come. Come home to romance—Silhouette Romance—for always!

Sincerely,

Tara Gavin
Senior Editor

ARLENE JAMES

A Man of His Word

Published by Silhouette Books New York

America's Publisher of Contemporary Romance

SILHOUETTE BOOKS
300 E. 42nd St., New York, N.Y. 10017

A MAN OF HIS WORD

ISBN: 0-373-08770-5

First Silhouette Books printing January 1991

Printed in the U.S.A.

Books by Arlene James

Silhouette Romance

ARLENE JAMES

grew up in Oklahoma and has lived all over the South. In 1976 she married "the most romantic man in the world." The author enjoys traveling with her husband, but writing has always been her chief pastime.

Chapter One

"Aunt Cori?" Dolly asked, rubbing her bright green eyes with small fists.

"Hmm?" Corinne slid her gaze from the road to her niece and back again. She knew, of course, what the question would be. Dolly had been asking it for over fifteen hundred miles, but her seemingly bottomless patience with this six-year-old cherub prevented irritation.

"How much longer?" The words came out on the tail end of a yawn. A smile curved Corinne's full, rosy lips.

"Well, that depends on whether or not we stop for dinner. You hungry?"

She looked back to her niece's roundish face, struck once again by the glow of that pale skin against the dark sheen of her hair and the vividness of eyes so big and green they put her in mind of lily pads. The little chin went up and down, and the big eyes widened. A feeling of love so deep and full and possessive that it was frightening, seized Corinne, and for a moment she was unable to respond, her heart in her throat. How had she come to love this child so completely in so short a time?

As the only child of her only sister, Dolly had been a significant part of Corinne's life since the day she was born. Premature, tiny, with black wispy hair and a face that was mostly eyes, she'd caught Corinne's heartstrings from the first moment and held on to them. But over the years—which had brought a succession of unhappy marriages for her sister, Martina, and a series of progressively more challenging jobs for her—Dolly had remained a significant but distant part of Corinne's life. Not that Corinne hadn't thought of her little niece often and regularly—and for good reason.

Martina had never been a particularly stable person, and the birth of her daughter had done nothing to bring about that stability. Her marriage to Dolly's father hadn't lasted even as long as her pregnancy, and though her other marriages had lasted longer, none had lasted as long as two years. Between men, Martina had been alternately despondent and sorrowful, but never so despondent or so sorrowful that she couldn't scout around for the next likely prospect, of which there seemed to be a limitless supply. The last one had even had money, but Martina had been foolish enough to sign an ironclad prenuptial agreement and so had double losses to grieve, the man and his fortune. This had been too much for Martina, so much so that she'd delivered Dolly to Corinne's apartment unannounced and left her.

That had been ten weeks ago. Since then, much had happened. She'd obtained legal guardianship of the child, her only condition for accepting the little moppet, had been through three baby-sitters and two pediatricians, had experienced her first child's birthday party, had drunk a bathtubful of pretend tea-party tea and had had the life scared out of her repeatedly because sweet, delicate Dolly suffered from asthma. In a very real way, it was Dolly's asthma that had put them on the road to Texas.

The first attack had come only three days after Dolly had arrived. In her ignorance, Corinne had had no alternative but to call the paramedics. The entire experience had been harrowing; but at least she'd known what to do the second time. Unfortunately, the baby-sitter had not, and the detailed instructions Corinne had given her over the telephone had gone right in one ear and out the other. In desperation, she'd called the paramedics once more, then frantically rushed home only to find the baby-sitter in hysterics and Dolly, alone among strangers in the back of an ambulance, on her way to the hospital, where she'd stayed for four days, her asthma having been complicated by bronchitis.

During that next month, the bronchitis had returned three times. Hardly a day had passed that Dolly didn't wheeze and cough and gasp. Corinne had missed a good deal of work, what with baby-sitters coming and going and Dolly's illness complicated by the lingering winter weather of New York. She'd learned early on that access to day-care centers was restricted by the demand for their services. Now she was learning how difficult it was to choose capable, reliable private help—and to appease a boss who had hired her, expecting her job to be her primary concern. It didn't help that all the other engineers working on this particular project were either single men or married men with wives available to look after their children. Already, she'd lost two particular design tasks to "less encumbered" fellows, and it had been suggested that she might want to transfer to a "less demanding" project within the company. The problem had been that no "less demanding'' project seemed to have a spot for her. Then had come another of Dolly's asthma attacks.

The timing now seemed providential, but at the moment it had appeared nothing short of disastrous. It had been the second week in March, the week the company had set aside for what it called "career training enhancement." This "enhancement" had consisted of a series of seminars conducted by experts from outside the company, many of them borrowed from noncompeting firms from as far away as Japan. Monday night of that week, however, Dolly had awakened from a nightmare. What she had dreamed remained a mystery, but the emotional stress, coupled with a case of the sniffles, had triggered the asthmatic symptoms. Corinne had dealt with the situation effectively for the first time, though it had taken more than one application of the inhalant, but it had been hours before Dolly had again drifted off to sleep, and by morning she had been running a temperature. Corinne had spent day two of the seminar week in the pediatrician's office. Her boss had been in no mood to hear or care about the extenuating circumstances; so, despite grave misgivings, Corinne had left Dolly in the care of the new sitter that next day and gone in to attend the seminar. She couldn't have been more shocked to see Jerry Arnold, the only serious boyfriend she'd had during college, standing behind the microphone.

What had followed still amazed and dazed her. For starters, she'd had words with her boss, who seemed incapable of understanding her predicament, and lunch with Jerry Arnold, who was as charming and adorable as ever. The boy wonder had done just what everyone had always said he would: at thirty, he was recognized as being at the top of his field and one step away from a vice-presidential job with a well-known and highly respected engineering firm based in Houston, Texas. Tall, tan, blond, fit and supremely self-assured, he had immediately encouraged her to come to Texas.

In the beginning the idea had seemed ludicrous for more than one reason. She hadn't seen Jerry Arnold since shortly after his graduation from college. They had parted by mutual consent. Jerry had been anxious to storm the "real" world of business, while she had only her sophomore year to look forward to. She'd heard later that he had married. In New York, he'd told her that he was divorced. "The price of ambition, I'm afraid," he'd said, but there'd been nothing flippant or lighthearted about it. Still, she couldn't see herself involved with Jerry, not romantically and certainly not professionally. Besides, Texas was so far away. He *had* tried to change her mind. In fact, during dinner at her place one evening he'd even enlisted Dolly's support, mesmerizing the child with stories of the Gulf Coast beaches and the new house he'd recently leased for himself and his mother on Galveston Island, south of Houston. It did sound lovely, especially with Geneva Arnold there to welcome them. Cori remembered Geneva with a special warmth, and she'd felt great sympathy for her when she'd heard how painful and debilitating her arthritis had become. Jerry had made it clear what a help she could be to his mother. Nevertheless, the idea of pulling up stakes and heading south with a child in tow seemed irresponsible at best.

After a few days, Jerry had returned to Texas. Shortly thereafter, the New York weather had taken a turn for the better, and for a while Cori had been able to put Jerry Arnold completely out of mind. Then one morning the babysitter had called to say she couldn't come in, throwing Cori into a panicked search for a replacement and, when it had become obvious that she wasn't going to succeed, helpless resignation. By noon, Corinne had found herself without not only a baby-sitter but a job, as well. That evening, when Jerry had called, Texas hadn't seemed so ludicrous, after all.

Still, she'd never expected to be doing this. Corinne Terral was not the sort to give up her career, her apartment, her friends or her freedom, on a whim. But then, that little bundle of pink sitting there with her dark hair hanging in her eyes was no whim. She was a flesh-and-blood child: a needing, giving, loving little person so hungry for attention and approval that she established instant rapport with almost every adult she encountered. Such a child must have the protection and understanding of a mature, stable guardian. There would be other jobs, better apartments, new friends. And what was a certain measure of freedom compared to the satisfaction of nurturing a human being? She had to laugh at herself. She was beginning to think like the original earth mother, but she wasn't completely without ambition or personal goals; there would be a forty-megabyte hard-disk computer with a color monitor, multifunction keyboard, mouse and appropriate software waiting for her in Galveston, and she had every intention of using it. Jerry could help her with that. All she needed was a list of East Texas companies that used contract design services and a couple of introductions and she'd be in business. She hoped.

She wondered how soon Jerry would be going down to South America, and felt an immediate prick of guilt for hoping it would be soon. She almost wished he hadn't been so obvious about his intention to revive the old romance. That was another reason for the guilt. She really didn't think Jerry was the man for her. She'd gone for the Greek-god type in college, the supremely confident handsome-and-knew-it type. But she had to give Jerry a lot of credit;

he had lived up to the promise of his potential and he'd done it in a field where his looks were far less of an asset than many others he could have chosen. Also, he had matured. There remained very little of that cocky adolescent she used to find so adorable. He still knew he was better-looking than ninety-nine percent of the men in the world, but that knowledge now seemed incidental to the fact that he was also a very capable and ingenious engineer with a gift for managing people as well as equations. It occurred to her that he'd managed her pretty well lately; but in the next instant, she put that idea out of her mind.

This was a perfectly reasonable and balanced arrangement, she reminded herself. Jerry was going to South America to work. Geneva's arthritis had gotten to the point where she was truly incapacitated by it. They had recently moved to a new house in a new community and been unable to find a suitable live-in care-giver. Who better to step in and help out than an old friend, especially an old friend for whom Geneva Arnold had demonstrated a particular fondness? This way, she could be there for Geneva as well as Dolly. They'd keep a roof over their heads, and the warmer climate would help to control Dolly's asthma. By the fall Dolly would be ready to enter kindergarten and Geneva would have found the help she needed. Then Corinne could get back on track with a full-time position somewhere. She and Dolly would be on their own once again, with neither Geneva nor Jerry the worse for it. Now that, she told herself, wasn't just a mutually beneficial arrangement; that was an answer to her prayer.

"Aunt Cori?" a little voice said, stopping her thoughts right there.

Corinne smiled. "Yes, love?"

"Can we have bisketti for dinner?"

She couldn't stop that first bubble of laughter from popping out and had to bite her lip before replying. "We had spaghetti for dinner last night. Besides, this close to the coast, we ought to find some pretty yummy seafood."

"We could have shrimps bisketti!" Dolly said hopefully, and this time Cori didn't even try to contain her laughter.

"We'll see what we can find when we get to Texas. It won't be long now."

"We're almost there?" Dolly asked incredulously, betraying as much disenchantment with the experience of road travel as eagerness to reach their destination.

"We'll spend the night in Beaumont," Cori decided suddenly, "and drive on down to Galveston in the morning. How does that sound?"

"Great!" Dolly said. "But what about our shrimps bisketti?"

Cori gave up to the scandalous impulses this child created within her. "I guess we could have spaghetti two nights in a row. But you have to promise to eat a nice salad."

Dolly wrinkled her pert nose, but she'd put on a brave smile to go with it. Cori laughed again and caved in all the way.

They turned in early that evening, replete with "bisketti," and rose in the black hours before dawn the next morning, hoping to beat the rush-hour traffic on their drive through Houston. They ate breakfast on the way— fresh fruit and yogurt washed down with orange juice. Corinne thanked God that Dolly didn't hate *all* the things that were good for her and drove on, a sense of excitement and expectation rising in her.

They hit Houston well before daylight. She'd known the traffic was supposed to be bad, but she was surprised at the number of cars on the streets at that early-morning hour. By six o'clock, when she stopped to call Jerry to warn him of their impending arrival, the rush of cars heading south on the interstate highway was thick enough to truly impede their progress, which was taking longer than she had expected. He assured her that he would be there when they arrived, but by seven she began to worry that he would have to leave for the office before she reached the house. Another forty minutes passed before they found themselves crossing West Bay, the narrow neck of water that separated the island from the mainland.

Dolly spotted a colorful sail off to her right, and her interest picked up significantly. She moved to the edge of her seat, straining against the safety belt, and giggled delightedly at the stilted houses flanking man-made waterways, which she dubbed "water streets."

"Look," Cori said, calling her attention to the tall stack of an enormous tanker slowly plying the waters of the wide Galveston Bay to the east. Dolly gasped and boosted herself higher by sitting on her foot.

"That's a big one!" she announced solemnly before settling down into her seat again. "Mommy showed me them afore," she went on, her tone matter-of-fact.

Corinne felt a pang of fear and regret. What must she think, this delicate child, about being separated from the only parent she had ever known? Did she miss Martina? Did she long for her mother's touch? She seemed so content and loving, so accepting of the careful explanations Cori had given her; but who knew, really, what thoughts went through her mind? Oh, how she hoped she had done the right thing, bringing the child to this place.

Within minutes the highway had turned into a city street. She had written down Jerry's directions and glanced at them often, but somehow none of the street names he'd given her were showing up. Either that or she was too taken by the squat palms and the faded elegance of buildings constructed a century ago to watch attentively. Many of the old buildings had fallen into decay, but many others had been restored and reclaimed for one use or another.

Before she knew it, they had reached the seawall. Dolly exclaimed over what looked like a small carnival occupying one corner of Stewart Beach Park. There were few people on the beach at that hour, but several runners were taking their daily constitutional on the broad seawall itself, which was paved over and fixed with park benches. Cori took her bearings and turned west on Seawall Boulevard. They glimpsed pebbly beaches and white caps on one side, every sort of building imaginable on the right.

Many of the buildings in this area were run-down, some were even vacant, but most seemed filled with the kinds of businesses one always finds in a tourist area. There were banks of tandem bicycles and surreys awaiting rental, cheap souvenir stands, ice-cream shops, bakeries, convenience stores. Soon, however, the clutter of small businesses gave way to the broad vistas of hotels and restaurants, each seemingly more prosperous than the last. This, too, yielded to arguably bigger and better things— vast expanses of polished new condominiums and resorts. Terraced and landscaped, they seemed to cover the island like prickly pear, mounding and falling in their own man-made hills and valleys, until suddenly they ceased. So did the view of the ocean, and without warning or apparent reason, Seawall Boulevard had become Termini Road, or so the road signs said.

They had entered the state-park area with its low, sandy grounds, inlets and bayous. The seawall gave way to natural beach, much of it overgrown with spiky grasses and marsh scrub. They passed occasional signs advertising concessions renting everything from jet skis to horses. Cori carefully pointed out these things to Dolly, receiving a variety of blank looks and barrages of questions in return.

Termini transformed itself into San Luis Pass Road, and there was the battered little sign pointing the way north to Oystermile Bayou. *The next right,* she reminded herself. *Narrow dirt road. Barbed-wire fence. The old windmill.* She spotted the windmill first. It looked like something from Holland, only with blades instead of sails, each slightly turned to catch the gulf breeze. To her surprise, it was working, and as they drew nearer, she saw that several head of sleek, fat cattle were gathered about the water troughs at its feet. Well, they were in Texas, after all, she reflected philosophically. Dolly thought it the funniest scene she'd ever seen and begged to be allowed to stop and pet the cows. Cori laughed and promised she'd try to arrange something later, explaining that cattle were not pets.

"We're almost there," she said. "Almost home!" *For a while, anyway.* But she wouldn't think of that just now. Dolly sat up very straight, trying to take in everything with her big eyes.

The car slowed and turned onto the sandy, gravelly road. The tires threw up a dusty cloud behind them as they headed north. The cows drank lazily and lifted their dripping noses to watch the car go by.

"Moooo," Dolly said wistfully, then she and Cori laughed.

There were trees, real trees in clumps all about them, and acres of tall, pale grasses. They passed an old, delapidated house, its shutters askew, the roof caving in over the wide verandas. A sea gull strutted across the overgrown yard, the solitary resident. Vacant houses invariably depressed Corinne, but she fixed her eyes on the road ahead. A half-mile farther on, the road turned into a real street with curbs and gutters but no sidewalks.

"Looks like we're here," she said cheerily. Dolly peeked out her window, then turned a puzzled face to her aunt, for she saw nothing on her side but an empty field and puddles of dark blue water. Cori laughed. "On the left, second house, and—" she brought the slowing car to a complete halt at the corner of the drive "—my word!"

Dolly struggled to lift herself from the seat, straining to see. Cori slid the gearshift into Park and quickly unbuckled the safety belt. It retracted instantly, and Dolly popped up on one knee, her arm sliding naturally about her aunt's neck. It was quite a sight. The grounds had been cleared of all but the ornamental cacti and the squat, wild palms, around which was an intricate, winding border of stone and a gravel walkway. Above this imaginative display towered a pair of leafy, moss-draped shade trees, the species of which Cori did not know, and several tall palms. In the midst of all this, cozied up nicely to the bayou, its terraces and decks spread out behind, stood the house.

"It's huge," Cori said.

"And ugly," Dolly pronounced flatly.

Corinne slid her a mildly censorious look, then turned her attention back to what was presumably their new home. She tilted her head to get a different perspective.

"It's not ugly, really. It's . . . modern and . . ."

"Gray," Dolly said.

Corinne swallowed. "Gray*ish*," she amended. "Why, it's almost silver, the way the siding has weathered. And look at all the different patterns and shapes."

Dolly said nothing, but her wispy brows were arched
pointedly above her green eyes. Cori took another hope-
ful look. The house resembled a pile of geometric shapes
stacked haphazardly against one another, with windows in
the cracks where they didn't quite blend. Built on tall pil-
ings hidden almost entirely by a broad, sweeping, U-
shaped staircase, it poked and strained and stabbed at the
sky, a rather aggressive, demanding, but confident structure. A tall, wide door made of slanting planks opened at
the apex of the stairs, and Jerry stepped out onto what
amounted to a narrow ledge, his dark slacks and white
shirt providing sharp contrast to the dull gray of his house.
He held on to the handle of a briefcase with one hand, and
seemed poised to descend the stairs when he spied the little car idling at the edge of his drive. He stared, then rose
on tiptoe, waving his free hand in welcome. Quickly he
deposited the briefcase on the top step and turned to the
wall beside the door. Stooping slightly, he seemed to be
speaking into a gold box. It was, apparently, an intercom.

Like it or not, Corinne told herself, *you're home, so get
on with it.* She smiled encouragingly at Dolly, who sank
into her seat, and put the car in motion. Jerry was already
trotting down the steps, his sleek blond hair falling forward over one eye. She reached the end of the drive before he reached the bottom of the stairs and had just a
moment to clasp her hand over Dolly's.

"I'm sure it's lovely on the inside," she whispered.
"We're going to like it here, I promise. You'll see."

Dolly smiled, the wisdom behind those enormous eyes
pricking Cori's heart. She put a finger to her lips im-
pishly, as if to say that she would be very careful not to in-
sult Jerry about his house. Corinne wanted to hug her, but
just then Jerry appeared at her door, shouting greetings
and laughing. Cori opened the door and got out, a bit

startled when Jerry threw his arms about her and kissed her quickly on the mouth. She'd expected a more sedate greeting, but there he was grinning like he'd just pulled off an enormous coup.

"God, I've been so worried about you! Was it a miserable drive? How wonderful to have you here at last! Hurry in. Mother's beside herself."

She tried to answer but gave it up as he ushered her around the front of the car to the passenger door. He let Dolly out and made an extravagant bow as she slid down to the ground.

"Someone is waiting to meet you," he said, straightening.

Dolly looked up at him with eyes that seemed to fill her face. "Hello, Mr. Arnold," she said solemnly.

He laughed aloud, as if she were a particularly fetching toy. "Hello, you little angel. You're as pretty as your Aunt Cori. Did you know that?"

"We look very much alike," she answered in that grave tone.

"I should say you do!" He hurried them forward.

They began to climb. It was a murderous staircase, the risers too narrow and too high. They were barely halfway up when Dolly began to flag, but she seemed to be concentrating very determinedly, and Cori let her go on. Jerry slowed to accommodate her and gave her a cheer when she'd reached the top. Once there, however, she turned to stare grimly down the way she'd come.

Jerry laid a hand to the back of her neck. Dolly turned back and gave him her hand, and three abreast they went through the door. The entry was pristine, the planking sanded smooth and sealed to protect the natural blond glow of the wood. Hand-painted Santa Fe style pots sat against each wall, and the vines growing from them had been fixed to the walls and even the ceiling, so that the passageway was covered in amazingly neat greenery. Dolly walked through it with her mouth open and her head slowly turning. Corinne disciplined a smile and followed briskly.

Jerry Arnold's house was certainly something. What wasn't planking was sand-colored carpet or glass. Fortunately, the interior was big and roomy, with a minimum of clutter and an abundance of light and air. The furnishings were unobtrusive, expensive, and provided a comfortable backdrop for the occasional bright splash of color from a painting or rug.

Geneva Arnold arrived, supported by a sleek white cane, the handle of which was a carved duck's head with a brass beak. Her delicate hands were gnarled and red, and she stood slightly stooped, her handsome face composed against complaint. The face itself, except for the added lines, was exactly as Cori remembered it, small and round with high, flat cheekbones and a wide, mobile mouth. Her short, soft hair, once the same buttery yellow as her son's, had gone completely white, the effect of which was that her pure blue eyes sparkled like gems. Yet, Cori saw a blankness in them that troubled her.

"Mother." Jerry bent low to place a kiss upon the woman's cheek. Geneva smiled benignly, then turned that same smile to Cori.

"Corinne, my dear, how exquisite to have you here." The two embraced, exchanging those endearing greetings that come with renewed acquaintance. "You're more beautiful than ever," Geneva complimented when they'd separated. She turned her attention to Dolly, who stood patiently to the side. "Oh, my goodness, who is this enchanting child?"

Corinne was astonished. She glared at Jerry, her eyes accusing him of not informing Geneva of Dolly's existence. He coughed and cleared his throat, turning slightly to bring his mouth close to her ear.

"It's the medicine," he whispered. "Affects her mind."

Geneva, meanwhile, was trying to entice Dolly. "Come here, child, and let me kiss you," she was saying. "It's difficult for me to move, you see, but I do so love little girls."

"Mother," Jerry said soothingly, "this is Cori's niece. Her name is Dolly. I told you about her, remember?"

Geneva looked up suddenly, a whimsical expression on her face. "What a silly I am!" She laughed merrily, turning back to the child. "It's Dolly, isn't it?" To Corinne, she said, "My land, she's the image of you. It's uncanny." Dolly, who had come to her as she spoke, put both arms around her and gave her a careful squeeze, those enormous emerald eyes glittering with natural compassion. Geneva gushed with laughter. "Oh, I'm so glad to have you both! What fun we'll have together!" She bent as best she could and dropped a kiss upon Dolly's brow. The effort was obviously painful.

Corinne's eyes misted with tears. Suddenly she was very glad she'd come, and she had the warm feeling that she couldn't have done Geneva Arnold a better turn than to have brought with her little Dolly. Everything was going to be all right. This was going to work out well, after all, for everyone. She'd have breathed a sigh of relief except that it would have given away her initial anxiety—and come too soon, for at that moment Geneva Arnold straightened, tears glittering in her jewel-blue eyes.

"Who would have thought it," she said, her words ringing dramatically off the cool, pale walls, "after all this time? I'm so thrilled that you're to be my daughter-in-law!'' And she wrapped her arms about the patient child, leaving Corinne to stare at Geneva's son in shocked silence.

Chapter Two

"Cori, darling, I didn't tell her any such thing! I told Reese. Mother merely overheard! I explained it to her, but you can see how she is. The doctors say it's partly her age and partly the pain medication. She's not so bad, really, once you get used to repeating yourself. Most of the time she makes splendid sense!"

Cori threw her hands up and continued to pace, working out her anger. "She's not the one I'm worried about! Jerry, whatever possessed you to tell *anyone* that we're getting married?"

"But I didn't tell *anyone,*" he insisted. "I told *Reese.*"

She halted and rolled her eyes. "Oh, well, that's different!" she said mockingly. "After all, he's not a real person. He's only your boss!" She put her hands to her temples, struggling to make sense of this mess. He had told his boss they were engaged! She couldn't believe it.

"You have to understand," he was saying. "Reese Compton is a very conservative, old-fashioned kind of fellow. I mean, he lives by this perfectly archaic moral code. How did you expect me to explain you, for Pete's sake? And with a child in the house, yet.'' He folded his arms and leaned against the gleaming white counter. The whole kitchen, in fact, was spotlessly white, from floor to ceiling to fixtures, with teakwood for molding and door handles in the shape of little shells. Like the rest of the house, it made a strong but tasteful statement about the occupant's life-style: rich, exceptional, simple.

Corinne sighed, feeling trapped and helpless—and oddly betrayed. ''What was wrong with the truth?'' she insisted. ''You met an old friend, temporarily unemployed and with a small child to support. You were having trouble finding someone to care for your mother, and you're on your way to South America. It's the perfect answer to both dilemmas!''

An uncomfortable look came over Jerry then. He stared at the floor, only glancing up at her fleetingly, and took a deep breath. ''The thing is...'' He paused to clear his throat, and a feeling of absolute dread seized her. ''It isn't working out exactly as we planned it.''

Cori stared at him. ''And what, exactly, does that mean?''

''Well, it's the Brazilian project. It's sort of hit a snag.''

Cori closed her eyes. ''You're not going,'' she rasped. ''Dear heavens, you're not going, and you don't need me here at all!''

She thought she was going to cry, thinking of that grueling drive and little Dolly's resigned patience at being uprooted yet again. How smug she had been, planning out this new life for them, and first thing there was this perfectly hideous house that would probably give the kid nightmares, and then poor Geneva with her arthritis and slightly scrambled brain, and now she was supposed to be engaged!

"Oh!" She sniffed, and Jerry pushed away from the counter and came to put his arms around her.

"It's not like that!" he assured her. "It's just that I don't know *when* I'll be going. It could be a few days. It could be a few—weeks. And meanwhile I had to justify our living here together."

"Rot!" she said into his shirtfront.

"Not exactly," he went on without missing a beat. "But not one of my brighter schemes, either. Nevertheless, Mother still needs someone she can count on. In fact, I don't really think you can take care of everything by yourself. I'm still looking for some day help, maybe a combination cook and housekeeper."

"Then why the lie?" she demanded, and Jerry shook his head in exasperation, holding her at arm's length now.

"Cori, you don't know Reese Compton. The man's as much an eccentric as a genius. He makes his employees sign contracts promising to conduct themselves, both privately and publicly, and I quote, 'in a manner fully above reproach.' You wouldn't believe the questions he asked me about my divorce! Why, until a few years ago, the policy at Compton Engineering was to hire *only* married people. Then, I don't know, his wife died somehow, and I guess he realized that single people can be as decent and honorable as anyone else. The point is—"

"The point is—if he's half as strict about this as you say he is, he's going to expect us to get married!"

"No! I told him that Mother needs you here now, but that we don't want to plan a wedding until after the Brazilian project is wrapped up."

"And that satisfied him?"

That uncomfortable look crossed his face again. "Not exactly."

Cori stiffened. "What does 'Not exactly' mean?"

He lifted his broad shoulders in a shrug and put on a sheepish smile. "It means, I'm not as smart as I thought I was. It means, Reese being Reese, both archaic and generous, he's offered me a room at his place until the Brazil trip is on again." Corinne spun away, smacking herself in the middle of the forehead with the heel of her hand.

"This is a bad dream," she said. "I'm not even here. I'm sitting beside the road somewhere hallucinating!"

"I couldn't very well turn him down," he went on as if she hadn't even spoken. "He lives just next door, you know, and since he's a friend as well as my boss—"

"Friends don't lie to one another!" she snapped.

"Without very good reason," he amended calmly. "Look, it's tricky being friends with the boss, office politics and all that, and Reese Compton isn't the easiest fellow to get to know."

"But where there's a will there's a way," she quipped caustically.

He looked wounded with a sort of practiced air. Nevertheless, she felt a stab of guilt. He was her benefactor, after all. He sighed, hands spread resignedly.

"All right. I admit it. I'm ambitious, and being friends with the boss has certain rewards, as well as problems, but I'm not the only one to benefit. There's Mother. I am her sole support." *And now yours and Dolly's,* came the silent reminder. "And there's Reese himself," he went on. "You know what they say about it being lonely at the top, only it seems doubly so with Reese. I suspect it has to do with losing his wife as much as that stiff-necked Compton code of honor. The thing is, if I tell him the truth now, we're both going to lose a friend, and he can't afford to lose me any more than *we* can afford to lose him.

We. He couldn't have made his point more solidly. She swallowed her pride, muttering, "I don't like this."

"Neither do I," he assured her. "But it needn't go on forever. After I get back from Brazil, we can just say we made a mistake and call it off. No one has to get hurt or embarrassed or anything. What do you say?" He smiled hopefully.

Corinne steeled herself, capitulating, and sent a daggered look at Jerry Arnold. "Do I have a choice?"

His smile was crooked. "Darling, you won't regret it, I promise you," he said cheerily. "And besides, most of the inconvenience will be mine. All you have to do is smile, keep quiet, and wear this." He fished out of his pants pocket a few pieces of change and extracted from them a slender gold ring set with what appeared to be a large, emerald-cut diamond.

Cori stared at it, pinched there between his thumb and forefinger, and at last sighed, reaching out for it. He dropped it into her hand, smiling broadly.

"Good old Cori," he said when she'd slipped it onto her finger. "I knew you wouldn't let me down!" He swept her into his arms, lifting her briefly off her feet. "It's going to work out well for us, Cori. You'll see." His grin was infectious, disarming, and as she looked up at him, Corinne found herself remembering another time when she'd have been thrilled to think of herself as Jerry Arnold's fiancée. But that had been long ago, and she had been another person almost entirely.

Jerry's hands rested lightly on her upper arms. Those blue, blue eyes felt warm on her face, and he stood so close that a deep breath would have brought his white shirtfront into contact with the soft fabric of her blouse. She thought, *if I just stand here, he'll kiss me.* But even as she thought it, she knew that wasn't what she wanted. Perhaps she was only angry or tired, but she didn't think so.

She stepped away, smiling feebly, and looked around the room. This wasn't for her. It was nice, just as Jerry was nice, but it wasn't for her. He wasn't for her—or for Dolly. She took a deep breath.

"I can't tell you how I appreciate this," he said softly. But she shook her head, feeling guilty for finding this so distasteful.

"I'm the one who should be grateful," she told him haltingly. "For Dolly as well as myself. But Jerry, this can't go on forever. We have to clear this up before too long."

"Yes, yes, of course." He smoothed her dark hair and lifted her chin with a curled finger. "As soon as possible, I promise. Everything's going to be fine. You'll see." He kissed her quickly on the tip of her nose and strode away. "I have to get going. Reese promised to send the helicopter back for me, and it's probably sitting over there right now with the rotor whirling."

"The helicopter?" she echoed, slightly confused.

He paused in the doorway, his grin blatantly prideful. "You know what they say—The bigger the boys—"

"The bigger the toys," she finished for him. "And I wondered how you bore the traffic!"

"That's just the idea," he said, giving her a wink. "Um, Mother can show you the extra rooms. Take your pick. Oh, and get some rest, love. We're expected for dinner at some friends' house tonight."

"Oh, Jerry!"

He lifted his hands innocently. "What could I say? They're anxious to meet you. Besides, they're first-rate people. You'll love them. Honestly."

She just put her hand over her eyes and groaned. "Is this it? Have you got any more surprises for me?"

He scratched an ear. "No, I think that's it."

"Ooh!" She gritted her teeth impotently, and he did what he'd always done in like circumstances: he laughed and left her, whistling as if he hadn't a care in the world.

Corinne dropped onto a painted chair, her head spinning. How had this happened? Why hadn't she known it couldn't be as simple as it had seemed?

"Oh, God," she said, "don't let this be a disaster!"

Early on, the portents were mixed. Dinner that first evening went fairly well, but Corinne couldn't help thinking of little Dolly alone in the house with Geneva, who most times seemed perfectly normal but at others as if she'd just awakened in a brand-new world. Jerry's friends were, as he'd said, quite sweet, but Corinne couldn't make herself relax into this role of fiancée, so by silent pact they made an early night of it, pleading exhaustion. Jerry seemed pleased with the way the evening had gone and left her at his own door with a light kiss upon the mouth, saying that he hated to be a bother but that she ought to prepare herself for Reese, who was sure to want to meet her at first opportunity.

Such turned out not to be the case. Reese Compton, it seemed, was a very busy man, and for that Cori felt gratitude. There were, after all, other things to worry about. The computer she'd ordered had somehow gotten lost in transit. The first cook Jerry hired left the third day without explanation, and Dolly badly stained the rug in her room with grape juice, which she had disobediently carried from the kitchen. About such things, however, Jerry was most understanding.

"Problems that can be solved with money," he said, "are not problems at all." Then he proceeded to have the carpet ripped out and replaced with a nice patterned vinyl and scatter rugs, which Dolly professed to like "most well." Cori was impressed but a little troubled, for this was a new attitude, at least so far as her experience with Jerry Arnold was concerned. Nevertheless, she was grateful, and she had cause to be so again soon.

She mentioned to Jerry one evening how concerned she was about finding the right doctor for Dolly. He sat down then and there and made a list of acquaintances with young children. Concentrating on those who resided on the island, he conducted a telephone survey all his own. The name of a certain pediatrician practicing out of the medical school on the eastern end of the island came up most often. Cori called for an appointment the next morning, and by week's end she was certain that she'd found the perfect children's doctor.

Jerry was not as happy. The novelty of bunking with the boss was wearing off. The Brazilian government seemed to be dragging its feet on approving the arrangements necessary to get Jerry's project off the ground, and Corinne found herself too caught up with Dolly and Geneva and the house to be much company—certainly not the ready date he'd apparently imagined she would be.

By the end of the second week, however, everything was beginning to smooth out. Jerry's project suddenly got the go ahead. They found a lovely middle-aged woman who was able to take on the cooking and housekeeping and anything else that should come her way, and in addition she seemed an extremely compassionate soul. Dolly and Geneva had become practically inseparable, though it was often a toss-up as to who was watching whom. The transport company had finally located the missing computer system, and life was finally showing signs of becoming what she had imagined it would be in Galveston. She was actually delighted when, the following Monday, she got in Jerry's slick BMW to drive him to Houston Intercontinental Airport, with a short side-trip to the office to pick up some important papers.

It was there that she got her first glimpse of Reese Compton. For all that he was their neighbor and Jerry's host as well as his employer, she had seen neither hide nor hair of the moving force behind Compton Engineering. He had been discussed at length at the dinner party to which Jerry had insisted she accompany him, and while the talk had been constrained by a respect so deep as to verge on awe, she had gathered from the general conversation that Reese Compton was not as well liked as he might have been. He certainly looked fierce enough standing there before the impressive granite and glass tower that housed his personal kingdom, his short, spiky ash-blond hair unruffled by a frisky breeze. His face, though curiously mobile as he talked with Jerry, seemed hard and craggy, as if sculpted from a ruddy brown rock. Standing just short of Jerry, he looked lean and strong in a pale gray suit conservatively but expensively cut, with a silver-gray tie knotted at the collar of a starched, blindingly white shirt.

After a few moments, Jerry glanced at his watch, and the two men started walking toward the car. Reese Compton continued to talk, Jerry nodding as he listened. Then, about halfway, they stopped. Compton nodded, and the two men moved off in opposite directions, waving as they parted. Within seconds, Jerry slid into the car.

"I hope you don't mind," he said, smoothing down his hair with his hands. "I asked Reese to look in on you periodically. I think he expected it, you know, being neighbors and all. Oh, and before I forget, I asked my secretary

to type a letter of reference and a list of leads for you, so
when the errant computer at last arrives, you can busy
yourself right away looking for work. You'll find plenty to
do, I'm sure of it."

"That's very good of you," she said, "and very good of
Compton, too—to look in, I mean."

Jerry grimaced. "About Reese," he said, "I wouldn't
mention the reference or the list. There's nothing improper about it, of course, but you can't be too careful
where he's concerned. I don't know how he's likely to view
it, so keep it quiet, if you don't mind. I've given Anne the
same word. By the way, she may mention something about
a bridal shower." He looked embarrassed and apologetic.
"As my secretary, she seems to feel those duties should fall
on her, since you're new to the area and friendless, as they
say. I told her it was too soon, but she's rather dogged
when she gets an idea into her head. If she brings it up, just
decline politely—and try not to feel too unkindly toward
me. *Please.*"

She wanted to snap at him that he'd put her in an awful
position, but she bit her tongue and forced a smile. The
man would be off to South America in little less than two
hours, after all, and as long as he was gone, she'd be pretty
much on her own. Having no friends in the area was a
boon in this case, because it meant not having to explain
this so-called engagement or act the part of the expectant
bride-to-be. She fully intended to be at work as soon as
possible, and hopefully on her own once again within a
very few months. By summer, she promised herself, and if
not by then, then by the time school began in the fall.
That, she had decided, was the goal: to be in their own
place by the time Dolly started school.

At the airport she left Jerry and his copious luggage on
the sidewalk with a skycap, then parked the car, walking

over to where he waited for her. The skycap was saying
something about paying extra duty with so many cases
when she arrived, and Jerry explained that he expected to
be gone several weeks, and that much of the baggage was
office material. He went through the same explanation
once again when he checked in, and would doubtlessly go
through it several more times before he reached his destination.

"Comes with the territory," he said as she walked him
to his departure gate. "Last year I went to Hong Kong,
and it was the same thing. Get Mother to show you the
slides of that trip, why don't you? She came over for a
couple of weeks. Perhaps, if this housekeeper works out,
you might like to come down for a visit this time, hmm?"

Corinne shook her head sternly. "No, I don't think so.
I wouldn't want to leave Dolly, not until we're perma-
nently settled, anyway. Besides, your mother's the one who
ought to get the invitation."

"Mother's traveling days are over, I'm afraid. She simply couldn't make such a trip alone in her condition. Perhaps the two of you . . ." He let the suggestion die away as
Corinne stubbornly shook her dark head. "I keep forget-
ting about the munchkin, don't I?"

"That's all right. She's got me to think of her."

"Lucky girl," he said, smiling wistfully. "You know,
Cori, it's not such a bad idea, the two of us."

She looked him square in the eye. "Isn't it, Jerry?
You're very sweet, you know, and you've quite literally
snatched my buns from the fire this time, but I don't think
we're so well suited anymore. We're all grown-up now,
Jerry, and somehow it just isn't the same."

He accepted this with a tilt of his head, but the gleam in
those blue eyes told her the matter was settled only temporarily. She felt she ought to tell him that it was hope-

less, but his flight was called just then, so she let it go. Swiftly, he gathered his valise and reading material and the little bag he'd packed as a precaution should his checked luggage be lost, kissed her, promised to call, sent love to his mother, kissed her again, and set off, disappearing down the long corridor that would take him to his plane.

Cori felt a vast sense of relief, tempered with a tinge of guilt, once he was gone.

How to do it? she wondered, looking at the box that occupied the passenger seat of her car. She should have thought of this before, but she'd been so excited when the freight master had called to say they'd located all components of the computer, at last, that she'd gone roaring off before she'd thought it through. Only now did she realize what a time she would have, getting it into the house by herself. She could either carry the box through the garage and up a narrow flight of steep steps to the kitchen, or she could lug the thing up that hideous stairway in front. Either way, it was going to be a big job for one person.

She elected, by virtue of sunshine, to go through the front. As much as she disliked the front entry of the house, she liked the claustrophobic feel of that stairwell between garage and kitchen even less. Every time she used it, she said a silent prayer that the single bulb in the overhead fixture would not choose that particular moment to go out. She could just imagine how it would feel to be caught with that enormous burden in a dark, narrow place, to be able neither to put it down nor turn around. The very thought made her skin crawl.

She parked at the side of the house, just before the open end of the garage, and lifted the trunk, exposing a trio of smaller boxes, which would also have to be carried up. She sighed.

"Serves you right," she muttered, pushing up her sleeves. She took the monitor up first—the lightness of the box belied by its girth—rang the bell, and waited for Geneva to come to the door. The wait was a long one, for Geneva moved slowly and painfully. She, nevertheless, greeted Corinne with a smile.

"Is there more?"

"'Fraid so," Cori replied, slipping inside to leave the box on the floor of the living room. Geneva clucked her tongue.

"That's the problem with this house. There's just no easy way of coming and going."

Cori nodded, wondering once more why Jerry had taken such a place, considering his mother's disability, but other matters required her immediate attention just then. She pushed the thought away and went out for the next load. This time she carried both the keyboard and the mouse in one trip, but she didn't take them inside. Instead, she left them on the landing and went back down to tackle the big part of the job. She was trying to work the box out of the car, and in fact almost had it, when she heard a male voice from behind her.

"Need a hand?"

The unexpected sound startled her for some reason, and she jumped. The box slid through her fingers, and she had to go down on one knee to keep from dropping it. He laughed at her, which, along with the near catastrophe he had just caused, produced a sudden flash of anger in her.

"For Pete's sake!"

"Sorry." He crouched over her and clamped his hands onto the box, taking its weight easily. His arms were very tan and defined with the bulge and bunch of much-used muscle. "I can manage this quite easily alone," he said. "If you'd just move out..."

Move out? Who did he think he was? It would serve him right if she let him lug the thing up by himself. Lips pursed smugly, she let go of the box, ducked her head and crawled out of the way. She struggled to her feet beside the car, cheeks burning with color, and turned to face her "helper," looking straight into the chiseled face of Reese Compton. It could be none other.

"I, um, thought you saw me coming across the yard," he said apologetically. He had an unusual voice, she noticed—quite deep and raspy; soft, yet oddly resonant.

"Well, I didn't," she replied tersely. He settled the box more firmly within his grasp.

"Jerry, ah, asked me to drop in," he explained. "Make sure everything's okay." She realized that he had an accent, too, a tendency to draw out the vowel sounds and all but skip the final consonants at the end of a word. It was charming; yet, from all accounts, Reese Compton was not a particularly charming man. He started suddenly, hiked up a knee, and balanced the box upon it, steadying it with one hand, while extending the other. "I'm your neighbor," he began. But she cut him off.

"Yes, I know, and Jerry's boss."

He nodded. "Reese Compton." He held his hand out to her.

She didn't know what else to do except take it. "Corinne Terral."

"Jerry's fiancée," he acknowledged, giving her hand a good shake before grasping the box again. She glanced away, hating the necessary deception, and managed to nod. "It's nice to meet you," he said. "It, uh, should have been sooner, but I hated to intrude. I mean, with Jer leaving so soon, I figured you'd want as much time together—alone—as you could get."

She gave him a weak smile. "Thanks."

He nodded, and she noted that his hair was a most unusual color, not gray but not brown either, and surprisingly thick. His brows were thick, too, but light—lighter even than his hair. And his eyes were palest blue and rimmed with brown, spiky lashes. Beneath his tan, his skin was ruddy and even a little rough in places, and the line of his jaw and chin bore the deep shadow of an especially heavy beard, though he stood cleanly shaved before her. He inclined his head toward the house, and she switched her gaze, stepping forward. He turned and fell in beside her, the box safe in his grip.

"I understand you have a little girl with you," he said conversationally, and she gave him a genuine smile.

"Yes, my niece, Dolly."

"I imagine she's too young for school," he went on, his speech as unencumbered as if he were sitting instead of carrying a large, heavy box across sandy ground.

"Yes, she is," she answered readily. "She could have started kindergarten this year, I suppose, but my sister didn't bother to enroll her. Marti's not much of a mother, frankly."

"That's tough," he said. "But at least she's got you."

"Yes, she does," she allowed proudly. "I couldn't love her more if she were my very own."

He nodded as if he understood completely and changed the subject. "So you're a computer buff."

She hesitated, blinking at him. "I beg your pardon?"

He stopped and pointedly looked down at the box. "This isn't exactly your garden-variety PC."

She laughed, understanding his conclusion, and turned to face him. A cool breeze blew her long, dark, shiny hair over her face. Thoughtlessly, she pushed it away with both hands.

"No, it isn't," she acknowledged with a smile. "Didn't Jerry tell you about me?"

"He told me about the little girl and about you two going together in college," he said. "And he told me you were quite lovely—which I find something of an understatement, if you don't mind my saying so."

Mind? she thought, beginning to like this man enormously. What woman would mind being complimented by an intelligent, virile... She abandoned the thought right there, managed a polite smile, and said simply, "Thank you." But an awkwardness had come over him. His gaze no longer met hers, and those thick brows were drawn together in a deep crease, his mouth a tight line beneath a slightly heavy nose. He looked positively stricken, and she felt a sudden need to rescue him from whatever impropriety he imagined he had committed. "Ah, about the computer," she said quickly, remembering and consciously skirting Jerry's warning. "I'm an engineer, you see, and I hope to work on contract. That way I can be home with Dolly at least until she starts school."

He seemed to seize the topic with a kind of relief. "Sounds workable," he commented brightly, carrying the box. "Jerry could help you with it, too. In fact," he said, striding past, "if he hasn't offered to set up a few contacts for you, I'd be glad to do it myself."

She turned and caught up with him, feeling light of step.

"What software are you using?" he asked.

She told him, adding, "I know it's no longer state-of-the-art, but it's still used so widely that I wouldn't want to take a chance on anything else. Of course, for the right contract I'd be willing to adapt."

"Good policy," he said. "Always keep your options open."

They reached the staircase, and not even Reese Compton could climb that man-made cliff with such a heavy burden and also carry on a conversation. She skipped ahead of him, reaching the door in time to open it and retrieve the lighter boxes she'd left on the landing before he made it to the top. He stopped there and took a deep breath. "Jerry's the only fellow I know who keeps in shape just by going in and out of his house."

"I know what you mean," she told him. "I already hate these stairs." She turned and led the way into the house, pausing by the door to wait until he'd passed through, then bumping it closed with her hip.

"Oh?" he was saying. "Does that mean you'll be moving after the wedding?"

Guilt assailed her. "I... We haven't discussed it." She hurried past him and turned left into the dining room. "This will do fine. I can manage from here."

"You sure?" he asked, lowering the box onto the tabletop.

"Very" was her reply as she placed the others beside it. She turned to face him, her hands going nervously to her thighs. "You've been very helpful. Thank you."

"Do you need anything else? I promised Jerry—"

"No. Nothing. Thank you again."

He inclined his head. "Anytime." Awkwardly, almost reluctantly, he turned to go. She followed him out into the entry hall. "You have my number, don't you?"

"I'm sure it's in Jerry's book," she said.

"Don't hesitate to call if you need anything."

"That's very kind, but I'm sure we'll be fine."

"All right." They were at the door now. Cori reached for the knob. "I'll check in again by and by."

She was about to say that he shouldn't bother but, of course, he was welcome, when a dull, single thump sounded from somewhere deep in the house. She listened, her senses alert, and had just dismissed the sound when—

"Aunt Cori-i-i! Cori! Quick!"

"Dol-*ly?*" She bolted down the hall, aware of Reese's presence right behind her. Her pulse rate tripled instantly.

"Aunt Cori!"

She turned into the living room on the left, certain the voice had come from the hallway dividing the bedrooms. Dolly ran to meet her, horror on her pale face.

"Geneva fell!" The child turned back the way she'd come, but before either she or her aunt could gain the hallway beyond the living room, Reese had pushed past them.

"Where is she?" Cori asked anxiously. Dolly was sobbing now.

"In my room!"

Reese was going from door to door and was halfway down the hall.

"All the way to the end!" Corinne called, picking up her pace again.

He went straight in. When Corinne caught up with him, he was bending over Geneva, who was on the floor, almost sitting. Beside her, the little stepstool of which Dolly was so fond lay on its side. "Easy now," Reese was saying.

"My wrist," Geneva whimpered. "So stupid of me!"

"It's my fault!" Dolly sobbed from the doorway. "I wanted the doll case down."

Corinne looked up at the shelf attached high upon the wall. One of six, it held those articles deemed least essential by Dolly only days before. She knew immediately what had happened. Dolly had wanted a case stored there for some reason. Geneva had attempted to reach it by stepping up onto the little stool and had fallen. Her right arm extended over her head, she had attempted to break her fall with the left. Reese was gently looking it over now. After a few seconds he looked up at Cori. His pale blue eyes said it all.

"Dolly," she said calmly, "would you get my purse, please, love? Geneva seems fine, but I think we ought to let a doctor decide." The girl disappeared at once. Corinne smiled down at Geneva, then looked at Reese. "We'll take my car."

He nodded. "She's pretty shaken. I'd better carry her."

Geneva herself began to weep. "It was all my fault," she said. "I knew better than to get up on that thing. A person just wants to be useful."

Cori shushed her as Reese gently gathered her into his arms and rose slowly to his feet. "Don't worry about that now," she said. "Just let us take care of you."

Geneva nodded, making a valiant attempt at a stiff upper lip, though she was obviously in pain. They went out, Reese with Geneva first. Dolly waited for them in the doorway to Cori's bedroom, Cori's brown bag clutched against her tummy. Corinne reached out and stroked her glossy head, and a little arm went immediately about her leg.

"It wasn't your fault," she told the child softly. "It wasn't anyone's fault, and everything's going to be fine. Okay?" Dolly nodded glumly, and Corinne smiled and reached for the bag, slinging it over her shoulder. "Let's go."

They went out together, running ahead of Reese to open the front door, then staying behind to close it. Down the stairs they went, hand in hand, hearing Geneva say, "I hope I'm not too heavy," and Reese's reassuring chuckle. When they got to the car, Dolly slipped into the back seat. Reese settled Geneva in the front and fastened her seat belt while Corinne fished the keys from her bag. Then they both strode around the front end to the driver's side.

"Do you know how to get to the hospital?" he asked as he opened the door. Corinne stopped dead, then thrust the keys at him in answer. He took them and stepped aside so she could raise the seat and get in back. "Glad I was here," he muttered quietly. Cori laid a hand upon his arm.

"So am I," she said. "So am I."

Chapter Three

First she put the magazine on his lap, then hiked her little leg and flung it across his knee, clearly expecting to be held. He was at once horrified and amused. Dolly was a pleasant child and a pretty one, and yet he felt himself recoil. The image of little Kenny hovered on the edges of his consciousness, but he ruthlessly turned aside and wondered instead how it was going with Mrs. Arnold. The poor old lady was a little daft but sweet, and he hated to think of her in pain—not that he had a chance, for young Miss Dolly was even then climbing onto his lap, determined to be read the captions on the political cartoons she had found in the center of the magazine.

Compliant but unsettled, he took the magazine into one hand and grimly allowed her to make herself comfortable upon his knee. It was most discomfitting—and so wrenchingly familiar. Again, he pushed away the memory of his son, concentrating upon the dark-haired little girl on his lap.

She squirmed and nestled and finally settled against the left side of his chest. He felt the weight of her head against his breast, her dark, glossy hair providing a thick cushion. She smelled of her own perfume, a delicate mix of soap and clay and crayon wax. *Not exactly sugar and spice,* he thought, but it was pleasant in a way. How long had it been since he'd held a child upon his lap? he wondered. But then, he didn't really want to think about that. No, indeed. Better not to think about that at all.

He smiled down at her. To his horror, she lifted a finger to her mouth, tilting her head back and gazing up at him as the stubby digit disappeared inside. Suddenly it all came back to him: Kenny, a squirming toddler upon his lap, that third finger clamped between his teeth as substitute for the pacifier they had first reluctantly given, then worriedly taken away. Kenny had never protested. Instead, he had merely taken to quietly sucking his middle finger, and they had likewise decided it was a rather charming foible for such a calm, bright, sweet-natured child.

Seeing the change of expression on his face, Dolly took her finger from her mouth and studied him. He made himself renew the smile and relax. Apparently satisfied, she smiled back and, just so there would be no misunderstanding about what she wanted from him, said, "I can't read."

He widened his eyes, feigning surprise. "What? A big girl like you?"

She shook her head solemnly, then brightened. "But I know my a'phabet."

He caught his breath, communicating doubtful admiration. "Is that so? Well, let's see you prove it." He brought the magazine around to face her and pointed to a letter. "What's this?"

She studied it for a moment.

"Umm. *H!*" He looked down at her, concealing his amusement, and hitched a brow in answer to her silent quest for approval.

Subdued, she dropped her eyes once more to the page, and her finger was returned to her mouth. She began to giggle. "That's not a *H!* That's an *N!*"

Her laughter was positively infectious, and he found himself chuckling along, repeating the game.

"Right you are. And what's this one?"

"*P!*" she crowed.

"Right again. And this?"

"Umm, *E!*"

He let the magazine fall away, teasing her. "My, but you're smart—for a *three-year-old!*"

"I'm not!" she protested good-naturedly. "I'm six!" She held up her hands, her fingers spread wide. One of them was slightly damp, but he ignored it, very much enjoying the game now. He made an outrageous face.

"Six! My goodness, you're almost a teenager!"

"I'm not!" She giggled.

He shook his head. "No? Well, then, you're almost old enough to start school."

She straightened and nodded enthusiastically, warming to this new subject. "Aunt Cori says I'll like school. She says I'm going to *pri*vate school."

"Is that a fact? And what are you going to study in private school, quantum theories?"

Her little face contorted. "No! Reading! And numbers!" She laughed heartily at his obvious stupidity, drawing up her chubby knees.

"What? No tickle me?"

She collapsed against his arm, laughing merrily while he waited with delicious anticipation for her to ask. She didn't disappoint him.

"What's tickle me?"

"Tickle you?" he teased. "Okay." Lightly, he waggled the tips of his fingers over her ribs. In an instant she became a squirming mass of giggles. He wrapped his arms about her in a protective hug, making certain she wouldn't fall to the floor, and blew a kiss against her cheek.

"Getting a bit restless, are we?"

The sound of the adult voice brought the romp to a sputtering end. Reese looked up, the smile still on his face, while Dolly went limp in his arms. Corinne Terral struck a tense pose, arms folded, dark head cocked to one side. Mercy, but she was a beautiful woman, he thought. Just the sort a Jerry Arnold would be lucky enough to find. He still wondered about the rapidity with which Jerry had gotten himself engaged, then reminded himself that this couple had actually known each other for years. Still... He dismissed his doubts, chalking them up to wishful thinking....

"How is she?" he asked, setting Dolly on her feet.

Corinne lifted a hand and smoothed her glossy crown. "Sedated. The break was just above the wrist, and the doctor says that's good. They're putting on a cast now. I have to get a prescription filled. Do you know which way the pharmacy is?"

"As a matter of fact, I do." He stood. "I'll get it, if you like. It'll give me a break from waiting."

She was looking at Dolly and smiling wistfully, a volume of love contained in that look. He thought of Gayla staring down at their son in his crib, and a lump rose in his throat. He cleared it, and immediately Corinne lifted her gaze.

"I'm sorry. You were saying?"

He smiled supportively. "The prescription. I'll be glad to take care of that for you."

"Oh, yes." She began digging in her pockets, drawing herself up tall and sliding her fingers into the slits on either side of her jeans. "Here." She handed over the folded slip of white paper. He took it gingerly, consciously avoiding touching her. It was silly. He hardly knew her. Moreover, she was engaged to marry another man, who was both employee and friend, not to mention neighbor. Yet, he felt oddly drawn to her, and that put him on his guard, as always.

He went right away to the pharmacy within the building and handed over the prescription to the blue-coated man behind the counter. While he waited, he drank a bottled cola purchased with quarters from a vending machine and tried not to think of Dolly or her aunt. He had a weakness for cola chilled in returnable bottles. It tasted cleaner and fresher than that packaged in aluminum and plastic and was ecologically superior, as well. Besides, it was a relatively harmless weakness, one which could be indulged without risk. No one's heart ever broke because of a lack of fulfillment of an acquired taste for bottled cola. He drained away the last of it just as the pharmacist returned to the counter with the prescribed vial of pills.

Feeling satisfied and even a little pampered, he quickly made his way back to the emergency-room waiting area. Along the way, he began to think of returning home. A fresh fillet of swordfish and an interesting new project proposal waited for him there. He imagined himself curled up in front of the fire with a glass of good wine at one elbow, his plate at the other, and the proposal open upon his knee. The night would be cool enough to justify a fire. It often was, thanks to the ocean breezes, even in summer when the days could seem unbearably hot. He reflected, not for the first time, that his life was a good one. He was in a fine, content frame of mind when he entered the waiting area.

Dolly was sitting on the floor, tracing around her hand on a piece of white paper with an ink pen. She seemed completely, even unnaturally, absorbed in this activity, not so much as glancing up when he came into the open room. A look at Corinne told him why. She was standing next to the wall, facing a tall, narrow window, and even from the back he could tell by the way she held herself that she was crying. He had come upon Gayla in just such a stance many a time, and every time it had cut his insides to ribbons, as it did now, though it was another woman whose tears brought the memories back. He stood awkwardly for a moment, wondering how on earth he'd gotten himself into this. In all the years since he'd lost them—first Ken, then Gayla—he'd managed to keep this from happening, and yet, here he was.

Damn! For a moment he allowed himself the luxury of regretting his friendship with Jerry Arnold. But he couldn't really blame Jerry. He'd known from the beginning exactly what sort of fellow he was dealing with. Jerry was *safe:* likable, intelligent, competent, but just unscrupulous enough to keep him from being too likable, and ambitious enough to keep him firmly in line. He was the right person with whom to play a game of golf or take a ride horseback along the beach. Besides, Reese told himself, he'd looked after the families of lesser men with less need for the sole reason that they worked for him and he knew their names. It was the decent thing to do. He believed in the decent thing, and just because these two made him think of those he'd loved was no excuse not to do it.

He glanced again at the child upon the floor and saw that she was watching him with a questioning expression.

"Someone ought to do something," that look said, "and it ought to be you."

He nodded and pulled a silent breath, then started forward like a hero heading for his own execution.

"I have the prescription," he said with forced lightness, to give her warning before rounding on her. She wiped hastily at her cheeks, her green eyes sparkling, and tried to put on a grateful smile.

"Thank you."

He stepped close, lowering and softening his voice. "Is something wrong? Is it Mrs. Arnold?" She was shaking her head, and he could tell by the stiffness of her face that she was embarrassed to have been caught with tears running down her cheeks. That made the moment all the more difficult for him. He tried to think what to say, finally coming up with "You must wish Jerry was here."

To his absolute confusion, she actually laughed. It came out husky and wry and abrupt. Seeing he was shocked, she hurried to justify the reaction.

"Oh. No. I'm sorry. It's just that, well, I wouldn't want to bother him with this. He'd worry, and, um, then I'd just worry about him worrying. You see?"

He nodded to be polite, but nothing she'd said or done made a moment's sense to him. Not even his own reaction seemed to make much sense; he felt like a chump, somehow. He ran his hands over the prickly ends of his hair.

"Is . . . is there anything I can do?" he asked lamely.

A truly apologetic expression came to her, and she reached out and laid a hand upon his shoulder. It was all he could do not to flinch. She smiled at him, blinking against the tears welling in her eyes.

"There's nothing to do!" she said. "It's my own silliness. I—it's kind of a pattern with me. I always manage to remain calm during a crisis. I don't know why, but I do.

And then afterward..." She lifted both hands in a shrug of helplessness, and it was only then that he realized he'd been holding his breath. "When there's no reason to—" she was going on "—I cry! Now, isn't that absurd? Isn't that the most...absurd..." Suddenly she lifted her hands and covered her face. He was stunned, appalled, confused, even—he admitted it—a little afraid, but then she sniffed from behind the mask of her hands, and he caved in like a wall of water.

"Here, now." He reached out before he thought, then hesitated just before his arm settled about her shoulders. He steeled himself for a shock and dropped his arm about her. She came immediately to lay her head upon his shoulder, dropping her hands. To his surprise, she felt warm and solid and human against him. He relaxed a bit and just let her weep, catching a glimpse of Dolly over the top of her head. For an instant, Dolly's big eyes, so like her aunt's, held his; then they turned away, and he fancied he'd seen a smile on her face. It unsettled him, and yet he had to admit that he liked these two. Jerry Arnold, he thought again, was a very lucky man, and Reese tightened his arm about the woman standing against him.

After a moment, she began to sniff and breathe deeply. With his free hand, he plucked a clean white handkerchief from his hip pocket and offered it to her, brushing it lightly against her cheek. She pulled away and took it. Head bowed, she sniffled and wiped until, dry again, she lifted her face.

"Thank you." She smiled tremulously. "Again."

He nodded and took his arm away. She stepped backward, putting some space between them, and lifted his handkerchief to her nose.

"All right now?" he asked, denying the impulse to touch her, to smooth the dark hair at her temple that had worked free to drift about her face.

"Fine," she said and drew a deep breath, holding aloft the handkerchief. "I'll launder this and return it to you."

"Don't worry about it," he returned automatically.

She lifted her chin, her eyes finding his, and smiled. "I don't know many men who actually carry handkerchiefs anymore. It's rather an old-fashioned custom, but a nice one."

"Well, I'm full of old-fashioned customs," he said. "Just ask anyone who works for me."

"There's nothing wrong with being old-fashioned," she told him. "I think it's sweet."

Sweet? He didn't quite know what to say to that, and he didn't like the way it made him feel, like a schoolboy with a crush. He felt his face begin to color. But just then, a pretty blond nurse in pastel green appeared and called out Corinne's name.

"I'm Miss Terral," she said, turning. The nurse smiled at her.

"Mrs. Arnold is nearly ready to leave. The doctor would like a word with you about her care and follow-up."

"Certainly." She went briskly to Dolly, stooped and stroked the child's silky head. "Can you play quietly a few minutes more, sweetheart?"

The girl nodded and lifted her face for a kiss. Corinne obliged, smacking her upon the mouth.

They're more like mother and daughter than aunt and niece, Reese commented to himself, and then the thought came that Corinne would miss that little girl when she left for her own home. He already felt sorry for Corinne, sensing what a wrench it would be for her to see the child go. *She'll need a friend,* he found himself thinking, and he

had promised Jerry he'd keep an eye out for her. With
Mrs. Arnold injured and Corinne being new to the area,
he'd really have to keep a close check, he decided.

She stood and turned to smile at him, fully composed
now, and steady as before. "I won't be long."

He smiled back. "Take your time. I'm in no hurry."

She sent him a grateful look, then left. He'd forgotten
all about the fish and the fire and the reading material
waiting for him. He'd forgotten everything but a promise
made in haste, which now seemed to have taken on a
greatly enhanced significance. But what was there to ponder, really? A promise was a promise, after all. And Reese
Compton was nothing if not a man of his word.

Corinne pushed the glass of juice away and drew the
newspaper closer, leaning far over the teak tabletop to
study the picture of Reese Compton. He was one of a trio,
the other two being the state governor and a Japanese trade
representative. The caption read: Houston Businessman,
Reese Compton, Signs Multimillion-dollar Partnership
Pact With Japanese Competitor. Governor Hails Model
Accord.

Intrigued, she carefully went over the story, taking note
of the many adjectives used to describe Reese Compton,
adjectives such as "conservative," "tough" and "loyal."
His contribution to a special state commission on eco-
nomic development was heralded, as well as his work with
Vietnam veterans and underprivileged youth. According
to the writer, Compton's name recently had been bandied
about in conservative political circles as that of a possible
candidate for a variety of offices. Reese himself, however,
went on the record with a statement that made it clear he
had no personal political goals whatsoever. He believed,
he'd said, that he could be much more effective by giving

his time to individual projects rather than holding office. It was all very interesting and informative, but by far the most intriguing section to Corinne was a single paragraph that seemed to cap the personal analysis. It read:

Not yet forty, Compton, successful and widowed, is considered to be one of the state's most eligible bachelors. His name has been paired with those of a number of women, including heiress Claudia Belgrado, councilwoman Linda Grandy and musician Nance Cooper. Yet Compton keeps a low social profile, surrounding himself with a small and elite circle of friends who shield him from public exposure. Known for his penchant for secrecy, Compton keeps all the best professional gossips guessing about his private life. Such inscrutability would seem at odds with the life of a political servant and may be the reason behind Compton's lack of political aspiration.

She reached for her juice again as she pondered what she had read. An heiress, a councilwoman, a musician. Reese Compton evidently liked a woman of substance—correction, *women* of substance. But was there, she wondered, a particular woman who enjoyed his attention?

It was none of her business, of course, but she couldn't help being curious. The man was a neighbor, after all, and a most conscientious neighbor, at that. Jerry could not have left them in better hands. But the man was a mystery, and the more she knew of him, the more mysterious he became.

She thought how helpful he'd been the day of the fall, how tenderly he'd ministered to Geneva; how quietly he'd assumed the care of Dolly, and how naturally he'd played with her; but mostly she remembered how safe and gentle and comforted she'd felt in his arms. He was a uniquely attractive man, one of those whose total somehow exceeded the sum of his parts. From all that she'd heard of him—and she'd heard of Reese Compton long before Jerry had mentioned his name, as had everyone else in her field—she hadn't expected to like him, to find him so accessible and, yet, so... enigmatic.

In the days since, she'd had time to observe him closely; for Reese was not a man to take his perceived responsibilities lightly. He'd dropped by almost every day to check on them, and the days he hadn't come, he'd called. Twice now, he'd had word of Jerry to bring them, and as she was without friends of her own, he'd served as a much-needed social outlet for her. Not that they were anything but friendly acquaintances at this stage. Their conversations had been about engineering and the possibility of her doing some consulting for Compton's; about the unbelievable Houston traffic and the amenities available on the island—all topics as innocuous and innocent as the weather. Yet, Corinne couldn't help feeling that she'd made a loyal and trustworthy friend. Under different circumstances...

But it was a moot question. As far as Reese Compton was concerned, she was engaged to marry Jerry, and it was loyalty to Jerry that had made him her friend. Once again, she experienced that rush of impatient indignation that she invariably felt when she thought about this sham engagement Jerry had forced upon her. More and more, she was certain it was unnecessary. In fact, at times it seemed to make no sense whatsoever. But then she couldn't really be sure what Reese would feel about anything, and now that the lie had been put forth, it seemed prudent to play along until Jerry could extricate them both from it. Nevertheless it was a tiresome bore—a fact so obvious that even

Geneva sensed her discomfort. In her poor, addlepated mind, however, Mrs. Arnold failed to make the correct connection and told one and all how desperately Corinne missed dear Jerry. She had been told the truth in no uncertain terms, yet she clung to the fantasy of the engagement; and Corinne had given up all hope of ever making the poor woman understand the genuine circumstances.

Cori folded the newspaper and pushed it aside. She took a good deal of satisfaction in her morning paper, but she'd learned early on that if she was to see it intact, she had to get to it before Geneva did. It had become her habit, then, to rise early, start breakfast, and enjoy the paper on her own before anyone else got up and about. In the process she had formed a certain fondness for the kitchen of Jerry's unconventional house, the breakfast nook especially, where a plank-topped trestle table was situated against a bow-shaped window of clear, sparkling glass. She finished her juice leisurely, enjoying the pastoral view. This truly was a little oasis of calm in the storm of people that swarmed over the island. But even the calm had its limitations.

"Good morning!" Geneva's voice chirped. Corinne turned from the window and smiled. Geneva had her housecoat on wrong-side-out and was searching for the belt, a look of confusion on her face. Cori got up and helped her off with it, turned it right side out and helped her slip it on again. Geneva smiled benignly. "Thank you, dear. Everything's so complicated these days." She sat herself down at the table and sighed. "Why can't anything be simple anymore?"

Cori patted her on the shoulder. "You're just not used to this new model of wrapper," she said lightly. Geneva thought on this, then screwed up her face.

"I liked the old one better. Why can't I just wear the old one with the great big buttons?"

"Because the sleeves on the old one are too narrow to accommodate this," Cori pointed out, rapping gently on the cast covering Geneva's hand, wrist and forearm.

"It's not seemly for a woman my age to wear a cast," she said with obvious distaste.

"It is if her arm is broken," Cori said gently, and changed the subject. "I put some French toast in the oven a while ago. It ought to be nice and crisp by now. Want some?"

Geneva looked up and beamed a childlike smile. "Jerry just loves French toast. Wouldn't he be happy if he was here! You must miss him terribly."

Cori felt herself blanch. "Not as much as you do, I'm sure," she murmured, turning away.

It was not the last time the theme was hit upon, however. Several times throughout the day, Geneva made mention of Jerry and what a shame it was that he and Cori could not be together. Once she even admonished Cori not to forget her son, saying, "I mustn't let you put him out of mind, but how could you, when you miss him so!" It was all very odd, and Corinne began to suspect that Jerry himself was somehow behind it, but then, too, it seemed quite harmless, and she didn't want to invent reasons to be dissatisfied. She had no way of knowing that Geneva's preoccupation with the notion of Jerry and herself as a couple would prove a catalyst of sorts.

She wasn't surprised when Reese dropped by just before dinner, still dressed in the light brown suit he'd worn to the office. The sound of the helicopter rotor was still audible in the distance when she opened the door to let him in. That continued to amaze her—the idea that anyone actually commuted by helicopter every day—but she supposed it was no more unusual than the situation in which she currently found herself.

She led him into the living room, where Geneva and Dolly had appeared. Reese had become a favorite with both of them. They seemed to look forward to his brief visits as much as she did. They all took seats, Dolly claiming a place next to Reese on the couch, Geneva and Corinne in flanking easy chairs.

Reese smiled at Dolly, then looked about. "Well, how are my favorite neighbors getting along today?" he asked. "Everybody okay? Anyone need anything?"

Geneva chuckled. "We're just fine, aren't we, girls? Fit as fiddles."

"No problems," Cori confirmed politely. "You really shouldn't worry about us."

"No bother," he said, his eyes steadily holding hers. After a moment he looked away. "I talked to Jerry today."

Geneva slid to the edge of her seat, her ankles crossed primly, her cast resting atop her knees. "Isn't he doing well down there in . . ." The name of the place suddenly eluded her.

"Brazil," Cori supplied helpfully, but Geneva looked doubtful. Reese sent her a conspiratorial glance, then turned his attention to Geneva.

"Of course," he said. "The exact location is Sorocaba, west of Sao Paulo."

Geneva brightened visibly. "Yes, that's it! Sorocaba. He says it's very picturesque, but I thought he sounded rather homesick, didn't you?"

Reese disciplined a grin. "Well, he didn't say anything about it to me. Naturally, we concentrated on business."

"Well, naturally," Geneva trilled. "That's why he's there in . . . Socoraba, er, Scrocorobi. . . ."

"Sorocaba," Reese corrected gently, and Dolly added matter-of-factly, "Brazil." In the instant of silence that followed, Geneva lifted her hands, cast and all, to her cheeks. An angelic smile lit up her face, then abruptly left it.

"Poor Cori," she said to Reese, her hands floating downward. "She doesn't like to talk about it, but I know she misses him terribly. He's worried about her, you know. He told me so. He's always asking me if she's enjoying herself, if she's seen anyone, gone anywhere. He worries about her." She sighed melodramatically.

Corinne was flabbergasted. She could feel her cheeks burning, and she simultaneously imagined the lie was written all over her face for Reese to see and wondered what Dolly was making of all this talk of Geneva's. She started to stammer.

"D-don't b-be silly," she managed, but Geneva was not to be silenced.

"Now you know you haven't been out of this house since Jerry left here," she said, next addressing herself to Reese. "She hasn't been out of this house, poor thing. Don't you think she ought to get out of the house?"

"Well, yes," he began, but whatever else he might have said was lost to Geneva's sudden enthusiasm.

"Oh, you're such a dear!" she exclaimed. "I knew we could count on you to get our Corinne out of the house. Jerry's so worried about her. She misses him so."

Reese began to fidget uncomfortably. Cori realized her mouth was ajar. She couldn't quite believe what was happening.

"Geneva," she said carefully, "I'm afraid you've misconstrued . . . I'm not—"

"Tut-tut," Geneva said, putting on an offended expression. "No one thinks I understand what's going on around me, but I have eyes, my girl, and ears to hear with. Now you take my advice and let Reese treat you to dinner.''

"Geneva!" Cori erupted.

"Why, yes," Reese was saying. "I'd be glad to."

"Reese, that's not necessary," she protested, but Geneva was on a roll.

"Nonsense," she said to Reese. "Make her go."

"I've, uh, been meaning to talk to you about doing a little consulting for the company, anyway," he told her.

Cori wanted to crawl under the chair. She looked from one to the other hopelessly. "I can't leave you and Dolly alone!" she said to Geneva. "You…your hand's in a cast! Not to mention that we're imposing!"

But no one was paying her the least mind. Reese was saying that he knew this little Mexican restaurant down on the Strand where they could take their time and talk, and Geneva was tut-tutting again and declaring that Mrs. Campbell, the housekeeper, would stay and that Dolly should go and fetch her right away so it could be put to her. Without so much as a word, Dolly hopped down off the couch and went to call Mrs. Campbell to the living room, and Cori started to protest that she'd have to change her clothing to go out, but Reese said there was no need.

"We'll keep it casual," he said, and he stood and began to take off his coat. Mrs. Campbell came, hurrying Dolly along in front of her, and while Geneva triumphantly determined that the housekeeper would, indeed, stay as long as she was needed, Reese shed his tie and vest and methodically rolled up his sleeves.

Cori sat back in her chair with a sigh. She was lost, beaten by an inferior intellect, good intentions and the compromising tenacity of a ludicrous lie. Deep down she knew it even before Mrs. Campbell drew herself up, chuckled and confessed that she really had no reason to go home anyway.

"I'll just keep Mrs. Arnold and the little princess company," she told Corinne. "You and the gentleman go along and enjoy yourself."

"There!" Geneva crowed, adding illogically, "Our Jerry will sleep better tonight!"

Cori merely shook her head, looked up at Reese's kind, implacable face, and surrendered. "I'll get my bag," she muttered, rising to do so.

Having powdered her nose, she returned, and Dolly immediately came to her for a goodbye kiss, her little face turned up expectantly. Cori bent and hugged her and kissed both chubby cheeks. Dolly gave her a smile, and after a moment's hesitation, stepped up to Reese for like treatment. For just an instant Corinne thought he would pretend not to notice, but suddenly he was swinging the child up onto his hip and accepting a warm hug around his neck. He gave her a pat and sat her down again and reached at once for Cori's arm. Taking up his coat and vest and tie, he ushered her forward, bidding the others a goodnight.

Cori allowed herself to be propelled across the living room, down the entry hall and out onto the landing. Reese pulled the door shut behind them and took up his assigned place at her elbow once again. Cori looked down that outlandish stairway and thought of the day she'd first laid eyes on it. She recalled feeling that it was silly and unnecessarily complicated, even ridiculous. A premonition? she wondered. Or a mere impression?

She looked at Reese Compton, and he looked at her. Something told her he felt the same way. Then the corners of his mouth began to turn upward, and suddenly they were both laughing.

"The truth is, I wasn't much in the mood to eat alone tonight anyway," he told her.

"And there is that little business about consulting for Compton Inc.," she reminded him.

"Yes, there's that." He laughed again and slipped his arm loosely about her back, nodding to prompt their descent. "I hope you like Mexican food."

"It so happens I do."

When they reached the bottom and turned toward his house, the conversation was flowing effortlessly. They were friends out together for the evening, and the truth somehow seemed closer, or the lie just didn't matter for the time being, or something. Maybe even something special.

Chapter Four

Half the fajita fell onto her plate, but she was laughing so hard she barely noticed. "He didn't really," she gasped. "That dignified Japanese gentleman?"

Reese was hunched over his plate, his sides shaking with mirth. "I swear," he said in a low, conspiratorial voice. "I didn't know what to do. You don't just correct a traditional Oriental, especially not in public. I didn't want to embarrass the man."

"How did you handle it?"

"Well, there was a fellow sitting nearby who'd ordered a lobster, so I just gave the waitress a nod and a little signal, and she brought us each a rather large, paper bib."

She almost howled. "You put on a bib to keep from embarrassing that man?"

"I couldn't very well let him sit there with the tablecloth tucked up under his chin. He was honoring us by ordering traditional American food, but he'd heard all about the juicy American hamburger, you see, and he wasn't about to repeat the gaffe of a colleague of his and go around with a tomato blotch on his shirtfront all day. I suppose he thought wearing the tablecloth was the way to prevent it. I don't know what he thought his napkin was for."

She dropped the remains of her fajita and put her hand over her gaping mouth, laughing as silently as she could manage. After several moments she got a hold on herself, relieved to see Reese had done the same. "It's awful of us to laugh at him," she said. "The poor man was trying so hard to do what was proper."

"I know. I know," he said. "Just be glad you didn't have to sit there with a straight face through the whole thing. I'm serious. Some of the guys were barely hanging in there. One little snicker would have brought us all down. Talk about a potential international incident! Of course, after it was all over with, I mean—after the guy was safely on a plane heading back to Tokyo—we closed the door and laughed—*screamed*—for the better part of an hour."

That produced another attack of giggles, but she quickly routed it. Right about then, the waitress brought the check. Absently, Reese went to his pocket for his wallet, brought it out and opened it. In the process, the dial of his watch seemed to catch his eye.

"Holy cow," he said. "It's a quarter of ten."

Cori couldn't believe it. They'd been here just over three hours. And poor Mrs. Campbell was still waiting to go home. "I've got to go," she stated at once.

Reese nodded and quickly thumbed a bill from his wallet. Cori gathered her things, and they rose in that awkward crouch necessary to extricate oneself from a booth when the seat is too high and the table too low. Reese got out first, then took her arm as she slipped out beside him. His touch felt at once familiar and excitingly novel. It was as if she'd known him for a very long time, and yet, as if she didn't know him at all. He steered her forward, across the dark green carpet, down onto the polished floor crowded with tables, and up again to the tiled entry. On the way, they passed the waitress, and together they bade her a good-night. Then it was out onto the sidewalk in the cool evening air.

A chilling breeze was blowing off of the bay at their backs, and they hurried to turn the corner to get away from it. Cori shivered, and Reese put his arm around her. Suddenly she felt warm and protected. She smiled up at him in appreciation and felt an immediate urge to rise up on tiptoe and bring her mouth against his. It would have been the most natural thing in the world to do, and yet . . .

Reese dropped his arm and slowly moved away. Cori fell into step beside him, missing his warmth and wondering if he'd sensed her thoughts. He began to tell her about the Strand, the beautifully restored waterfront area through which they walked. Designated a National Historic Landmark District and carefully restored to nineteenth-century grandeur, it was a major tourist attraction on the island as well as a vital business center teeming with restaurants, hotels, unique shops, museums, even a theater whose productions regularly brought season-ticket holders from Houston. In addition, there were trolleys and horse-drawn carriages in which to ride, even a steam locomotive and a paddle-wheel boat, and at Pier 21, an 1877 Tall Ship, the *Elissa,* frequently docked and allowed sightseers on board to explore its decks.

"We'll have to bring Dolly down here," he commented idly. Then he quickly amended the statement. "*You* really should."

She nodded, hating the idea that she couldn't just invite this nice man to take an interest in her. But there was Jerry to consider. As ludicrous as this lie was, she'd agreed to it, and she did owe Jerry a certain loyalty. After all, it was Jerry who had brought her here and provided a home, however temporary, for herself and Dolly. She hated to think where they would be if he hadn't come along when he had with a solution. She just hadn't known the price would be so high. How could she have?

They reached the parking lot. Reese paid the attendant, put her in his Volvo and drove her home. It had been a lovely evening, a genuine delight, and she was sorry to see it end, but she didn't expect him to get out and climb those horrid stairs just to see her to the door, which he did, saying flippantly that it was good exercise.

"You don't look as if you really need any extra exercise," she told him as they drew near the top, but he merely smiled.

"Neither do you," he said, coming to a stop on the landing. "You're quite a lovely woman."

He looked away then, and Cori found herself thinking, *Now is when he'd kiss me, if this were a real date.* But real dates were out of the question as long as she had Jerry's ring on her finger. She'd have liked to have "accidentally" lost it in the sand, but as that would be too cruel, she'd just have to grin and bear it. She squared her shoulders.

"Well, thank you, for the compliment as well as a truly enjoyable evening."

"My pleasure," he said, turning a careful smile on her. Their eyes met, and for a moment it seemed they were both holding their breaths. Then suddenly his knuckles skimmed her cheek, and the smile he was wearing grew lopsided. "Jerry Arnold's one very lucky man," he said, and before she could speak, he had kissed her cheek and turned away, calling "Good night!" over his shoulder as he trotted down again.

"Good night," she whispered, trying not to hate "the lucky man" for making her feel that she was missing something, someone, very special.

"Sir? Sir? Mr. Compton!"

"Wha—?" Reese jumped. "Oh." He instantly realized what he'd done, and apologized. "I'm sorry, Denise, er, *Ms.* Fowler. My mind wandered."

"Obviously." The attractive young woman, tall, blond and slender as a reed, hid a smirk by using the eraser of her pencil to scratch the end of her nose. "Now, as I was saying, I want to put Global on the back burner for a while and concentrate on the Plumbline Manufacturing bid."

"And I," put in the gentleman opposite her, "have a deadline I have to meet on Global."

"But it isn't pressing," Ms. Fowler argued.

"Not yet!" he returned. "But it will be if you start pulling people off!"

"The bid takes priority. Or don't you want a job to go to when Global's over?"

"That's melodramatic!"

"It's not! If we fail to get in the bid—"

"Enough!" Reese declared, pushing his chair back from his desk. He templed his fingers and tried to concentrate for a moment on the problem at hand. It was not as easy as it should have been. He wanted to think of something else, *someone* else. What was it about Corinne Terral that wouldn't leave him alone? She was attractive, yes, and intelligent—but attractive, intelligent women were everywhere. One of them was standing before him, in fact, and he couldn't even concentrate on her when she was here shouting. He passed a hand over his face, exhaling slowly.

"All right," he said, making an instant decision and pulling himself forward again. "We're going to slack off Global for a bit." He held up a hand, palm out, before Carlton Cross could protest. Carlton was a good man, but Ms. Denise Fowler was right in this instance.

"How do we stand on Global right this minute?" Reese asked.

Carlton filled him in quickly and fully, and this time Reese managed to concentrate, but still Corinne wouldn't leave him alone. Even as he listened, she was sneaking into the back of his mind. Well, why not? They could be friends, couldn't they? After all, they had a good deal in common. She was an engineer, for Pete's sake! In fact, she was an experienced engineer looking for contract work. Unless he was mistaken, she might even be a solution to this particular problem. He'd have to check that out.

He smiled, then realized Carlton and Denise were staring at him oddly. He cleared his throat.

"How about this, Cross? We'll put an outside consultant on Global, an independent. She, ah, or he, can take up the slack for a while. We'll keep a close check, of course, but meanwhile, Ms. Fowler can have a couple of key people to help her group get the Plumbline bid on track. Agreed?"

Carlton nodded. "I can live with that."

Denise Fowler put on her gloating expression. She'd have been incensed to know it, but she was famous among her co-workers for that look, not that she was disliked for it. She usually deserved it. Denise was good; *very* good. Yet she and the boss were not friends. He didn't know why, but they weren't, which put the lie to the notion that he and Corinne should be friends because they shared a career choice in common.

But, dammit, he *liked* the woman. He didn't *dislike* Denise Fowler, of course, but he didn't like her, not as he liked Corinne.

What was it, he asked himself again as Cross and Fowler left his office, that made Corinne Terral so very...likable? *More like compelling,* he admitted silently; and only one other woman in his memory had been as compelling. Gayla. But that didn't help to define Corinne's attractiveness, because they were nothing alike.

Gayla had been helpless, in a way. She was very bright and could have done anything she'd really wanted to. It was just that she hadn't wanted to do the kinds of things most women were doing these days. She'd been content with the singular role of housewife, and she'd worked hard at making their home comfortable and appealing and orderly. He'd been concerned with building up the company then. He'd put in long, exhausting hours, and the one constant in his life had been Gayla. He'd always known that she would be there, soothing, comforting, encouraging. His dinner would be hot. The atmosphere would be conducive to relaxation, and she was a wizard at keeping things on an even keel. Somehow, no matter how empty the bank account, she'd always made sure their life-style hadn't suffered. A lot of the time it had just been a matter of adjusting the emphasis; but then they really hadn't needed much beyond each other. Gayla would have been content to simply sit within the circle of his arms and make interested comments while he went on and on about matters of business and home life. God, how he'd missed her! And he could admit now that it had begun when Kenny had come.

The changes had been subtle then. They were no longer merely two, yet Kenneth had been such a part of them that they'd had trouble separating themselves from him. Gayla especially had loved the role of parent, so much so that he had been jealous of all the time and care she'd lavished on their son. But there was Kenny to fill up any empty spaces in his life. What a joy he'd been! What a gift! They'd never expected to have children because Gayla's fallopian tubes had been scarred from a past infection. When they'd gotten that news, she'd been terribly upset, but somehow it hadn't mattered to him. He'd had her. If he'd needed anyone else, he hadn't known it. Then suddenly, against all odds, she was pregnant, and he'd been stunned by how deliriously happy he was about that. Having Ken had been an unexpected joy, and losing him had been so emotionally devastating that he'd wondered if he'd ever recover. Gayla hadn't.

It was that simple, really. After Kenny, nothing had ever been the same again. His loving, doting wife had become an empty, listless, grief-filled absentee. He had tried to help her. He'd given up everything else to be with her. He'd devoted himself to being the kind of loving, nurturing spouse she had been to him. He hadn't known what else to do, and no one had been able to tell him—not the counselors, not the ministers, not Gayla herself. Less than a year had passed before she, too, was dead. Officially, the cause of death was ruled an accident, a freakish, one-car accident; but in his heart of hearts, Reese had long ago accepted the idea that Gayla had taken her own life—and that he could have done nothing to prevent it.

Somehow he'd managed to go on. Somehow he'd even managed to be happy again, eventually. Once or twice in the intervening years he'd even fancied himself in love. Indeed, he'd worked at being in love for a while. Fortunately he'd realized his mistake before he could compound it by making a second marriage that would inevitably have failed. He doubted that he would ever marry again. He was happy now, just as he was. Why should he risk devastation again? He had everything he needed—the company, a home that was once again a genuine haven, money, influence, friends. Well, okay, one really never had enough friends. And this single life-style he'd chosen had its drawbacks.

Sometimes he sorely missed what he thought of as "female companionship," but he wasn't very good at moral indulgences. He supposed his ideas on that score were old-fashioned, maybe even archaic, but his sexual relationship with Gayla had been supremely satisfying, and that had taught him how valuable the old ideals were. As far as he was concerned, a truly fulfilling sexual experience required not only desire, but love, trust and commitment.

How strange that he should think of all that now, and all because an employee and neighbor had gotten himself engaged to a particularly compelling woman. He thought of their evening out: how she had looked, her little mannerisms, the warmth of her body when he'd touched her, the gusto with which she'd eaten, the sound of her laughter. Laughter. He smiled now, just thinking about it. He couldn't believe he'd told her that story about the Japanese official. It was not, after all, for public consumption. Funny as it was, feelings could be wounded—and relationships hindered—if the tale got back to the gentleman involved. Normally he wouldn't have repeated the story to anyone. Well, he'd have told Gayla. That was just the sort of thing he'd have shared with her. She'd had a way of making him want to talk, and he missed that feeling of being able to say anything at all with complete ease and trust.

Perhaps that was it. Yes, of course, it was. For whatever reason, Corinne Terral made him want to talk, to communicate, to share. She got to him in a way that no other woman ever had—save one. Suddenly he could see her in Gayla's place—by his side, on his arm, in his home, in his . . . Oops.

He got up out of his chair and paced across the floor. Now that was carrying things too far. Corinne was not Gayla. She had no place in his life, certainly not that of a wife, and she never would. Even if she did compel him to ponder the imponderables, he couldn't, wouldn't, do anything about it. She was engaged to marry Jerry Arnold; and Jerry was not only a neighbor and a friend of sorts, he was an employee and a good one. Whatever his own level of interest in Corinne Terral, she was taken. Period. No discussion needed. He liked her, but that didn't mean he could or should court her. *Court her?*

Damn. He was beginning to wish he'd never laid eyes on her. Certainly he regretted having agreed to this role of caretaker. But how was he to know what she was going to be like? How could he ever have predicted this attraction? Oh, what a predicament! Well, he didn't have much option. He wouldn't let this be a problem. He'd do his duty—and nothing else. Corinne Terral was a lovely, compelling woman, but she was Jerry Arnold's lovely, compelling woman, and he wasn't about to forget that—not for a moment. Not for a single moment.

He went back to his desk, picked up the receiver of his phone and punched a button. "Evelyn," he said, "I promised Carlton Cross an outside consultant for the Global project. Would you see that Personnel and Services gets the message, and, um, tell them to pull a name out of the file." He rotated his chair and gazed out the window, listening. "I know it's routine. I just wanted to make sure it was handled properly. Thanks."

He let his hand and the receiver in it fall away from his ear. He felt guilty as hell for not having had her name added to the file, but had he done so at this particular time, it might have been construed as a subtle indication that he wanted the Global project assigned to her—and that was just what he didn't want.

"Liar," he told himself. But then he turned away from the window and hung up the phone, because what he wanted didn't really count this time. Irritably, he pulled a folder from his desk drawer and went to work. What else, after all, could he do?

Corinne stretched out and dangled her leg over the arm of the easy chair in Jerry's den. She liked this room better than the living room. She liked the colorful area rug and the stained woods and the shutters on the tall windows. She liked the striped ticking on the big sofa and the dented cabinet of the television in the corner, and she especially liked the little shelf-lined nook with its version of the captain's desk hinged to the wall and its creaky wood chair on rollers. It was here that she kept her computer system and occasionally worked. So far, she'd done three small drafting jobs for a display-case manufacturer and a couple of elevation sketches for a local architect, and the truth was that she was bored to tears a lot of the time. She sighed, and like a fairy assigned to chase away the doldrums, Dolly appeared in the doorway.

"You want to play a game with me?"

"Sure." Corinne smiled, not because she really wanted to play but because she loved this child. That had become her reason for just about everything she did lately. It was, after all, her reason for even being here; and she had the comfort of knowing that the move had been good for Dolly. So far the child had not suffered a single asthmatic incident—a fact that Corinne attributed chiefly to the climate.

"I'll get it." Dolly went off to fetch a dilapidated box from her closet. Corinne hoped it wouldn't be Candyland. They'd been on a Candyland jag for days. Before she had a chance to find out, the doorbell rang. She got up, went immediately to the intercom and flipped the switch.

"Just a minute," she called into the speaker. Reese Compton's voice came back at her.

"No hurry."

She put her hands together in a silent clap and went off at a clip, unmindful of the fact that she was in her stocking feet.

"I'll get it!" she cried to whomever was within hearing distance.

It had been days since he'd stopped by, and she was beginning to wonder if he was leery of getting roped into another evening of providing entertainment for her. He had called, but half the time Geneva got to the phone first, and afterward, Cori couldn't make sense of the bits of conversation that were related to her. It was all very frustrating; she didn't even want to admit *how* frustrating, and she told herself it was only because she was bored. But she couldn't deny the tiny, fluttering thrill she felt at the prospect of seeing him again.

By the time she got to the front door she was breathless because she had hurried, but she didn't want to look as if she'd hurried, so she took a moment to smooth her hair and catch her breath. Then, very calmly, her mouth fashioned in a not-too-welcoming smile, she opened the door. He was standing with his back to her, gazing off across the grounds, his hands in the pockets of a pair of olive-green, pleated, twill slacks. Abruptly he turned. He was wearing a black T-shirt and an olive cardigan thrown over his shoulders with the sleeves hanging down over his chest. His smile was instant.

"Hi. How's it going?"

She felt herself relaxing, smiling. "Great. Come on in."

He stepped into the foyer with her, saying, "Where's the little one? She still here?"

The phrasing struck her as odd, but she didn't think too much about it. "As a matter of fact, she's probably in the den. We were about to play a gripping game of Candyland or Ping-Pong."

"Ping-Pong?"

She grinned. "Actually, I'm hoping for Ping-Pong. I'm about Candyland-ed out."

"Well, I am intrigued. Let's not hold up the match."

She laughed and led him along the hallway, across the living room, into a second hall, down a wide flight of eight or nine steps and, after a sharp left turn, through a doorway into the den. Dolly was kneeling beside a seaman's chest topped with glass and used as a coffee table. She looked up and smiled as they entered. The Candyland game board and all the little color-blocked cards were spread out on the glass top. Cori stifled a groan and sent a loaded glance at Reese, who lifted his arms in a shrug that seemed to say "Hey, what're you gonna do?"

"All right," she said, accepting the inevitable. "Let's get to it."

Reese, it seemed, had never seen Candyland played, and she was only too glad to offer him the opportunity to compete, but he stubbornly declined, only to get caught up minutes later trying to help Dolly win. It was all just a matter of drawing the right cards, of course, but between the two of them they managed to make Dolly think she was a master strategist. Before it was all over, Reese was down on the floor with her, sitting Indian-fashion while Dolly, who had appropriated his lap, occasionally forgot herself and bounced up and down on his crossed ankles. When they had at last managed to let her win, Reese made like a cheering crowd and carried her around the room on his shoulders.

After the victory lap, Cori suggested Dolly run upstairs and check on Geneva, who should have been up from her nap by now. She went off without a moment's hesitation, and they heard her calling out to Geneva as she reached the top of the stairs. "I won. I beat Aunt Cori, and Mr. Compton gave me a parade!" They laughed, and Cori collapsed into the easy chair.

"I shouldn't complain about playing with her," she confessed. "I know I'll miss all this one day."

"Yes, you certainly will," he agreed, coming to sit on the couch. "In fact, I'm not sure I could do what you're doing. I mean, you get so attached to them, and then they just go away."

"Yeah." She contemplated the day that Dolly, a grown woman, moved out on her own, and she felt herself getting misty-eyed. She crossed her legs, the pink knit fabric of her sweats stretching easily. "It's worth it, though. Look how happy she is. I'm so glad to have this time to spend at home with her, but . . ." She cocked her head to one side and reached up to give her bangs a lift with her fingers. "I need a diversion, something more adult than Candyland."

"There's always Ping-Pong," he said with a grin.

"I had something a tad more challenging in mind." She bit her lip, wondering if it would be presumptuous of her to ask the question she was contemplating. He gave her a level, interested look, and she decided to chance it. "Listen, have you had a chance to think about me doing some work for you?" His immediate reaction seemed one of wary surprise. She hurried on. "I can do the work, Reese, and I have letters of reference to prove it." She got up from the chair and moved toward the computer nook, talking fast. "I even have some drawings here that you might want to look at." To her relief, he followed her. "They're pretty simple, but I tell you what—why don't I boot up the system and show you what it can do?"

He took the elevation prints she offered him and glanced over them, saying, "I don't doubt your capabilities."

She heard a silent "but" hanging on the end of his sentence and grimaced, launching ahead. "Let me just hit this switch." She did so, and the system started up with a low-pitched whine that leveled off after several seconds. Reese still had a doubtful look on his face, but she wasn't giving up quite yet. She'd had to sell her skills before. She sat down and began to type commands into the machine. The program loaded, a series of blinking lights indicating the function.

"Okay. I've been working on a little project all my own," she muttered. "Let's see what you think." Typing quickly, she brought up the correct document, then scrolled the screen to show off the three-dimensional design from every angle.

"Hey!" He chuckled. "That's a jungle gym."

"Not quite," she said, taking up the mouse and touching it to the screen to enlarge a certain detail. "It's more like a portable playground. Look here. See that bivalve hinge? The whole thing's designed to fold up into a four-by-eight bundle, swing, slide, teeter-totter and monkey bars. And look at this." She typed in a few more commands, bringing up another picture. "I haven't worked all the kinks out yet, but I figure you can fold up a merry-go-round sort of like you would an umbrella. See?" She worked the mouse, and the legs on the pictured contraption began to flex as if they belonged to a mechanical octopus. "And when this piece is joined to the other..."

"You've got a real playground," he finished for her, bending over her shoulder to get a close look. "You know, you could add one of those forts to this thing, and I bet the full layout wouldn't take up more than . . ."

"Sixty point three square feet, maybe sixty point eight." She put the whole thing to scrolling again, and he watched with interest.

"You know, this isn't as simple as it sounds. I've seen military hardware with more primitive design than this. You ought to think about marketing this."

She laughed. "It's not quite ready for that, and I'm really only interested in something for Dolly that we could fold up and move on short notice—something I could then unfold myself, without needing a lot of tools and extra help."

"You mean something she could take with her when she leaves here," he commented idly, sounding a little confused. Corinne opened her mouth to say that he was right; but then it occurred to her that as far as Reese was concerned, she and Dolly were not supposed to leave here—at least not on their own.

"Er, not exactly," she hedged, quickly closing the document. "It's just an idea."

"But a good one," he insisted, straightening to stand beside her.

She could feel his knuckles through the double thickness of her appliquéd sweatshirt as he gripped the top rail of her chair, and suddenly she needed to put some distance between them. She kicked down the system and slid out of her chair. Quickly she detailed several of the projects on which she'd worked, emphasizing that she'd had experience in diverse areas.

"So," she wound up, trying to sound casual, "what do you think? Can Compton Engineering use me?"

He was still standing by the chair she'd just vacated, looking at her with an expression that registered somewhere between relief and resignation. "Absolutely."

It sounded absolute, yet something about it made her think twice. "Wait, now, I don't want to impose. In fact, I probably shouldn't have said anything. Jerry warned me that it might not be a good idea, and I certainly won't be offended if you agree with him."

"I *don't* agree with him. In fact, I have just the project in mind for you."

"Really?" She smiled because he suddenly seemed so sure. "You aren't just being nice?"

"Honestly," he said, coming forward to take her by the shoulders. "I thought of you the other day when this particular job came up, but... Well, now that I see how anxious you are to get started, I'll have P & S call you."

"P & S?"

"Personnel and Services. We keep a list of names, a pool of consultants, and I'll see that you get on it. Okay?"

"Okay. Great!"

He smiled down at her, and for a moment it seemed he wanted to say something more. His mouth was open, and his pale eyes studied hers intently, but then he apparently thought better of it, for he dropped his hands and backed away. "I, um, ought to go."

Dolly came clattering down the stairs then and burst into the room, shouting, "Dinner!"

Already? The time had flown—again. It always seemed to when Reese was around. Cori looked at Dolly, then at Reese, and she thought how the two seemed to enjoy one another. He had no one to go home to, had he? She said, "Why don't you stay? Mrs. Campbell's an excellent cook, and there's always extra."

"We're having shrimp bisketti!" Dolly announced happily. Cori laughed.

"She means spaghetti with shrimp sauce. It's her favorite."

"Sounds like you've got a pretty sophisticated palate," he said to Dolly, "but, I'm sorry, sweetheart, I can't stay."

Cori was truly disappointed, but she put on a smile before he looked up again. "That's too bad. Maybe another time."

"Maybe," he said, but she thought he sounded doubtful. She guessed he was uncertain how it might be interpreted. Everybody was always saying how old-fashioned he was. Maybe he thought it wouldn't look proper if he was known to be dining with another man's fiancée. But then that hadn't seemed to bother him the night they went to the Strand. On second thought, Geneva hadn't given him much choice that evening. It probably wasn't wise to assume he'd been comfortable with the idea. It probably wasn't wise to assume anything about Reese Compton.

She saw him out, thanked him for dropping by, and promised to give Geneva his best. As she turned away from the door, she had to wonder if she would ever see that project he'd mentioned. Well, if he thought that best, that's how it would have to be. She made up her mind she would never mention it again unless he did. But she didn't have to be happy about it, and now that he was gone, the day seemed more drab and colorless than ever—except, of course, for Dolly. She fixed her mind on that sweet little person who had come to mean so much to her, and went in to eat.

Chapter Five

Reese sat forward and pressed the lighted button on his intercom.

"Yes?"

"It's Carlton Cross and Miss Terral."

He smiled in spite of himself. God knew he hadn't intended to hire her, and there was no doubt that having her around all the time was sheer lunacy, but no one could say she hadn't done a damn fine job.

He wondered what had brought her to him this time. Hadn't she uncovered enough problems with the project already? He laughed just because she was good. Even Denise Fowler had had to admit that Cori was good. Every suggestion and change Corinne had made was right on target. Carlton was hot to hire her on full-time, and Reese had secretly begun to hope that eventually she would accept, even though she'd probably be married to Jerry Arnold by then. He couldn't help enjoying having her around. No law said he couldn't take pleasure in that. He pressed a second button.

"Thank you, Evelyn. Send them in."

They came through the door, laughing and talking, and strode across the floor, coming to a stop at the long, narrow desk that had once belonged to Sam Houston, first president of the short-lived Republic of Texas. Reese leaned back in his chair and clasped his hands together behind his head. *No problem here,* he judged rightly, but he was content to let the meeting unfold naturally.

"Afternoon, Top Gun," said Carlton, using the affectionate nickname coined by those closest to Reese at Compton, Inc. Reese nodded indulgently. Carlton turned to Cori with an explanation. "The boss was air force," he said. "Educated at the academy."

"No kidding?"

The look she settled on him frankly telegraphed that she was impressed. He felt a unique type of satisfaction, and for once he didn't bother to downplay the significance of this revelation. Something told him it wasn't necessary with Corinne. He was right.

"Flight training?" she asked, and watched a smile cross his mouth.

"Yep."

"Fighter pilot?"

"Nope."

"Ah." No censure, just understanding.

Had he made the grade as fighter pilot, he'd still be in uniform, and she sensed that. He wasn't ashamed of his service record. Indeed, he had a great fondness for the military, but he wasn't the sort of man to settle for anything short of the best from himself: the top spot. Had he made it as a fighter pilot, he still wouldn't have been satisfied until he'd made certain that he was the *best* fighter pilot in the air. At some point, he'd realized he'd need a war for that, and that was when he'd understood he was in the wrong business. He'd served out his hitch and turned his talents elsewhere, taking with him a healthy respect for those men in uniform. He was happy with the place he'd made for himself in the business world, glad he hadn't made the mistake of staying in the military, and content that those closest to him understood. How ironic that she should become one of them with such ease. This woman was not meant for Jerry Arnold.

He didn't know where that thought had come from, and he wasn't sure he even wanted to know, but something told him this engagement wasn't the usual sort of arrangement that a man and woman made when they were in love. Yet she wore Jerry's ring, and as long as she did, she belonged to Jerry. Period. Subject closed. Down to business.

"To what do I owe the honor of this visit?" he asked, and the mood abruptly but smoothly changed.

Carlton Cross put on a satisfied smile. "How would you feel about having the Global Project in, oh, say, six months under deadline?"

This was good news. Reese looked from Carlton to Corinne, taking note of the calm, confident smile of the latter. He felt an unjustified surge of pride. Leaning back, he linked his fingers over the gold buckle of his belt. "I take it the lady responsible for this extraordinary feat will explain."

She did so eagerly and succinctly, her frank, emerald-green gaze unswerving. In the end he couldn't restrain his praise.

"Well done! Eight or nine different engineers brainstormed that original concept and not a one of them expected implementation to be so simple. I applaud your good sense. There'll be a bonus in this one." He got to his feet and shook her hand.

She beamed her pleasure and pride, her palm cool and smooth against his. "I'd settle for another assignment."

"You'll get that, too," he promised her, reluctant to give up the feel of her hand within his.

"We could even do a little better than that," Carlton put in. "We could use you around here full-time." He turned to the boss, leaning against the edge of the desk. "Reese, let me put her on the San Antonio program. She's division-head material, I know it!"

Corinne's hand slipped from his before he even had a chance to turn over Carlton's proposition in his head. He sent his gaze back to her and found that an uneasiness had replaced the pleasure. He sat down again, rightly reading refusal in her eyes.

"I can't."

"Wait'll you hear what we want to do with this, Corinne," Carlton prodded enthusiastically. "This is the most exciting project in the house. Got a budget like the Pentagon's. We figure ten years for consummation. We're still seven, eight months away from implementation to phase one, so you'd be in on the ground floor. Trust me, this one's a career-maker."

Corinne's sleek, dark head dropped forward, and Reese could see she was agonizing, but after a moment she looked up again. "I'm sorry."

Cross opened his mouth, but Reese cut him off. "Carlton, leave us alone, will you?" A direct look stalled yet another protest and produced a wink instead. Cross excused himself, supposing the Top Gun was about to do a little private arm-twisting. Reese Compton could be very convincing, but in this case Carlton had misread his boss, which was precisely what Reese intended. When the door closed, he turned to Corinne with a half smile.

"No explanation needed," he said softly, and she relaxed with obvious relief.

"Thanks."

He waved away the notion of gratitude, seeing no reason for it. "How have you been?"

"Fine. Dolly sends her love."

He smiled and nodded. "And Geneva?" He watched her beautiful smile falter. He templed his fingers, alert to the most subtle of nuances. Cori took a deep breath, and he couldn't help noticing the rise and fall of her breasts beneath the pink silk of her blouse and the deep plum of her suit jacket. He made himself lift his gaze to her face. The skin was pale and creamy but tinged with rose along those prominent cheekbones. The natural dusky pink of her lips shone with a clear gloss, and delicate, feathery brows of sooty black curved in the gentlest of arches over deeply set eyes of a bright, arresting green. Wispy bangs swept her forehead in careful disarray, a charming contrast to the sleek locks falling neatly over her shoulders. He noted that she wore small earrings of pink glass roses set in clusters of tiny gold and silver leaves, and he thought, *If she were mine, I'd buy her emeralds.* But she wasn't his. The ring on the third finger of her left hand attested to that.

"Geneva's all right," she was saying. "It's just that she gets so confused sometimes, poor thing. The doctor suspects she might have had a small stroke a while ago, perhaps even a series of them. He's suggested therapy, and Jerry's asked me to arrange things through your insurance carrier. Will that be possible?"

"Of course," he said. "Leave it to me. I'll call down and have someone get in touch with you."

She turned on that dazzling smile. "What would I do without you?"

"Don't be silly," he came back, but the words were more for himself than for her. He was fighting a smile of his own, and his heart was beating double time. She wouldn't need him once Jerry returned home, but the fact remained that she needed him now. "So," he said, sitting forward, "about that new contract I promised you . . ."

For half an hour they discussed the possibilities. He offered her a choice of several interesting projects, but, as she pointed out, there were other employees to be considered, project managers, lead designers. In the end, she insisted that the decision should go through proper channels, a fact that pleased him greatly. But he warned her that reaching a decision could take a few days. "They'll be fighting over you once word gets out about your work on Global." She laughed and thanked him and said she'd get out of his way so he could work on something important. He told her that friends were important, and she told him that she'd never had a better friend or a finer one. He told himself that friendship was all there was to it, and not only for her, but for Jerry, too. He saw her to the door and promised to get back to her soon. What else could he do, after all? He owed it to Jerry. He had promised. And Reese Compton always kept his promises.

Corinne listened to the tinny voice coming to her through the receiver, her face implacable, for Dolly played at her feet, spoon-feeding a plastic baby imaginary applesauce, while Geneva stared at the television, straining to hear two conversations at once. Corinne was quite convinced that Geneva had expected this call and knew very well what its subject was. She smiled at Corinne occasionally, as if suddenly remembering to look innocent. Cori tried to take no offense. Jerry was her son, after all, and as a mother, Geneva was more vulnerable to manipulation than most. Corinne turned her thoughts from the mother to the son, listening carefully and forming her replies with an unemotional, well-modulated voice.

"Everything's fine," she said, once he'd paused to draw breath.

"Oh, really?" Jerry came back. "I don't think so. I think the potential is there for disaster. I don't like it, Cori. I don't like it at all."

"That's too bad," she told him lightly. "I'm really enjoying the work."

"There are other companies you can work for!" he insisted.

"I know," she said reasonably, "but I already have *this* contract."

"Get out of it!" he shouted over a sudden hiss of interference. The line crackled for several seconds, and in the distance a strange voice murmured unintelligibly. Cori waited until the line was clear again.

"I can't, Jer," she answered brightly, and in the unpredictable vagaries of modern telephone service, the line cleared so cleanly that she could hear his sigh.

"Cori, please think," he urged. "You could accidentally give away our secret."

"The lie, you mean," she retorted liltingly. "Well, that has to be cleared up anyway, doesn't it?"

"No. Not like this."

She heard the change in his tone and prepared herself for what was coming.

"It doesn't have to be a lie, Cori," he said. "It could be the truth if you'd just realize we're meant to be together."

"Hmm. No. No, I don't think so."

"I know so, Cori. Why are you being so stubborn? Don't you remember what it was like when we were together?"

"Obviously not the same way you do."

"You'd remember if I were there," he told her confidently. "I'd make you remember."

She knew it was meant to sound provocative, enticing, but even as she smiled and nodded to his mother, she fought the urge to hang up on him. Such conceit! Why hadn't she remembered *that* before she'd gotten herself into this mess?

"If you were here, Jerry," she reminded him sweetly, "I wouldn't be."

"Darling..." he began, but she cut him off, gaily changing the subject.

"Did you know that Dolly is taking swimming lessons?"

"Wh-what? Swim—"

"Yes, I enrolled her this afternoon. She begins Monday morning." She nudged Dolly with her toe and was rewarded with a grin full of tiny white teeth. She wondered just when a child started to lose her baby teeth and what the going rate was for the tooth fairy.

"That's good," Jerry was muttering.

"I think so. We're on an island, for Pete's sake. She needs to know how to take care of herself."

"Does that mean you're going to stay?" he asked hopefully.

"Where else would I go?" she answered. "Of course, I do have a standing job offer with Compton."

"Oh, God," he groaned. "You wouldn't do that to me, Cori, would you?"

She had half a mind to declare that she would, but she was partial to the truth, and despite everything, she did owe Jerry some consideration. "No, I wouldn't," she said. "I've already turned down the offer for full-time employment, but I've no intention of canceling my contract, Jerry. You have to accept that."

He muttered something unintelligible that she knew wasn't complimentary, but she chose to ignore it. Then, "Cori, please, you have to protect me. You know Reese now. You can see why I had to invent this engagement. Just give me a chance to end this gracefully. That's all I ask."

She knew Reese now, all right, and she wanted to say that what Jerry was asking was too much, but she couldn't do that, not with his mother sitting there trying to pretend she wasn't listening. Besides, it wouldn't help to confuse Dolly, who knew nothing—or at least very little—of what was going on. Still, she had to force the words out.

"A-all r-right. We'll go on as we are until—"

"Until I can get home and take care of everything in my own way," he finished for her. "God, Cori, you're incredible. Is it any wonder I want you back?"

"Forget that, Jerry," she told him tersely.

"I'll try," he said, using that provocative tone again.

"Fine. I have to go now."

"Don't you want to know how it's going here?" he asked, sounding hurt. Cori gritted her teeth and made an interested sound. He went on for several minutes about how the locals thought he was Einstein, about the new concept he had of the project, about the quaint local habits and the inexpensive price of domestic help. He ended by hinting that she ought to come down for a visit. "I'd love to show you the place," he said.

"I'm needed here," she replied shortly.

"Yes," he conceded, "of course you are. What would I do without you?"

"I shudder to think."

He laughed. The charm meter was registering maximum, and even Corinne herself was surprised by how unaffected she remained.

"Tell Mother I'll call again soon."

"I will."

"Remember our agreement."

"I *will*. Goodbye now."

At last she got him off the phone. She took a deep breath and exhaled slowly, relaxing, then delivered his message to Geneva, who peered at her anxiously, her gnarled hands trembling.

"Is everything all right, dear?" she wanted to know, and Corinne smiled compassionately.

"Everything's fine," she assured her. "Everything is just fine."

Geneva, too, seemed to relax. She beamed at Corinne. "Oh, that's good." She turned back to the television, leaning forward to hear more clearly. After a moment, she said to no one in particular, "Jerry's a good boy. He's really a good boy." She seemed to expect no answer, as if she had simply reminded herself of one of the basic tenets of her life. Contented, she settled into her corner of the couch to watch her program uninterrupted.

Corinne reached for the remote control and turned up the volume. Dear Dolly was humming to herself under her breath as she pretended to wash her baby. Cori smiled to herself, letting go of the last of her exasperation. Life was not so difficult, after all. There was Dolly, and the time they had to spend together. Geneva was sweet and docile, if a little doddering. Her work was rewarding and convenient. They had a roof over their heads and food on the table, thanks to Jerry, who was nothing more than a voice on the phone and a pesky inconvenience at the moment.

And there was Reese. Despite everything, she had to count him as one of her blessings.

But Reese was the one real problem, and she mustn't forget that. However much she would like to tell him the truth, she couldn't. She liked to think he would understand, for loyalty was one of his strongest characteristics, but she couldn't help feeling *disloyal* to him somehow, as perverse as that seemed. Or was it her heart that she betrayed with her silence?

Frustration returned, deep, dark and sharp. She did not love Jerry Arnold, but she must not love Reese Compton. Perhaps, for reasons he didn't even understand, Jerry was right, after all. She made herself a promise, a vow: she would not again seek Reese out. As far as work was concerned, she would deal with Carlton Cross exclusively. It had never truly been necessary to bring Reese into it to begin with, and she would drop that artifice right now. She would ask no favors, admit no needs, and she would see to it that he was not again maneuvered into playing the role of escort. They were acquaintances, nothing more, and she mustn't allow herself to believe anything else was possible. She set her mind to it, resolute, definite, resigned.

That resolution stayed with her throughout the remaining weeks of the month of May, and by June life had taken on a bustle that made it easier to keep. School was over. Community summer programs swung into gear. Corinne signed up Dolly for a variety of activities ranging from ballet to sand painting. They met new people, made new friends, developed a social life. Geneva, too, acquired new interests. Her therapy included meetings twice a week with a support group made up of people her own age. A core group formed, their needs as much social as physical. She hosted a tea and accepted a few reciprocating invitations. It was hard to tell if she was making any real progress, but she seemed happy. Although her mental condition remained muddled, she seemed a little stronger physically and complained less of pain, which was in itself worth the time and effort required to keep her in therapy.

Adding to all this relentless activity, Dolly developed a case of sniffles, which, though carefully tended, turned into an ear infection, requiring not one but two trips to the pediatrician and several to the pharmacy. After forty-eight hours of green eardrops, pink and red syrups and orange chewable pills, the fever and the pain were gone. All that remained afterward was relief that this episode had not developed into asthma. That alone was enough to strengthen Corinne's resolve—and after all this time living with Jerry's lie, her resolve definitely needed strengthening.

Between work, the infection, Dolly's schedule and Geneva's therapy, Corinne hardly had a moment to herself, but on the occasions when she did, she put on her sandals and shorts and a big floppy hat, slathered herself with sun block, then went to the beach, where she walked and watched the waves roll in. It wasn't crowded on their section of the island, which was protected and allowed to remain in a natural state, so that the beaches were narrow and clotted with stands of grass and scrub hiding choice chunks of driftwood and debris. Cori loved to explore. Even the disgusting clumps of squid and jellyfish intrigued her, for they were exotic and strange and new and so very incongruent with her own image of Texas. She took Dolly with her on occasion, and they made a picnic out of it. The water was cold, but they tiptoed in anyway and exclaimed together over the sight of fish arcing above its brown-green surface.

Even with all this going on, Reese still managed to occupy a portion of her thoughts and a small segment of her time. It wasn't possible to avoid him entirely. He still called to ask if all was well, but Cori provided him with stock answers, chatting about everything that was going on, scoffing at the idea of concern. She told him nothing that might elicit an offering of aid, omitting even Dolly's brief illness. As far as work was concerned, Carlton Cross acted not only as supervisor but also as go-between, and yet she could not avoid Reese entirely. There were times when he literally summoned her to his office, but she would arrive there only to find this congenial man smiling at her as he sat behind his narrow desk. He would issue a few words of praise, a few more of counsel, and a firm decision or two. He always thanked her for coming, inquired about Dolly and Geneva, and delivered a concise progress report on Jerry's project. She always felt a sense of relief—and disappointment, but she remained resigned to the idea that Reese Compton must remain a cordial acquaintance and nothing more. So it was with reservation, and surprise, that she received his invitation to the company picnic.

It was the Monday of the second week of June, and she had delivered some drawings and notations to Carlton and was on her way out of the building when the word came down from upstairs that Mr. Compton required a brief meeting with Miss Terral. She heard her name called over the paging system and reported to the nearest secretary, who made a call and reported the message that Mr. Compton was waiting for her in his office. She thought about making a quick escape, but it was already too late for that and she knew it. Steeling herself, she strolled to the elevator banks and went up.

Evelyn greeted her with a familiar smile when she entered the small suite of rooms that comprised Reese's office. She was shown in immediately, but Reese was not at his desk. He was helping himself to a soft drink from a small refrigerator concealed in a cabinet at the end of the room. He, too, smiled and waved her in, turning to pop the cap off of a bottle.

"Soft drink?" he offered, lifting the old-fashioned bottle high. She shook her head tersely. "I drink too many of these," he went on, walking over to the corner of his desk and inviting her to take a chair. "I'll probably have the weakest kidneys and the healthiest heart of all the old guys in the nursing home when I get there."

She sat down, uncertain how best to respond to this effervescent good humor. He perched on the corner of his desk, one foot swinging playfully. She noticed that he wore dark socks, almost sheer, and black shoes with his navy blue suit. His shirt was blue-and-white striped. In contrast, his tie was red with white paisleys, and yet it all worked somehow, right down to the small red silk square in his breast pocket. He looked very "put together," and for some reason that made her smile.

"Sure you don't want something?" he asked, but again she shook her head. "Okay," he said, "then I guess we'll just get down to business—except there isn't any."

She looked up in shock. "I don't understand."

He swallowed a gulp of soda and grinned. "Here you go," he said, reaching for a heavy pale gray envelope stood on end next to his telephone. He passed the envelope to her, explaining its contents. "It's an invitation to the company picnic on the beach this Saturday. We send them out to all our consultants and individual contractors. In-house, we just make an announcement and take a head count, but we like to handle our 'associates' with a bit more class." He took another long drink and let her look over the printed card inside.

She didn't really read it, but she stared at it a moment before looking up to say "Thank you."

He nodded and seemed to wait, as if expecting her to say something else. She tried to think, but the only thought in her head was that she shouldn't go, so she opened her mouth to say so; then suddenly he jumped in ahead of her.

"I'll, uh, pick you up about nine, okay? And how many should we expect?"

She just blinked at him. "How many?"

He nodded. "How many are coming? Who are you bringing?"

"Bringing," she repeated dumbly, stalling as his full meaning came clear.

"Geneva coming?"

"Uh, no."

"Dolly?"

"No, I don't think so."

"Well, then," he said, looking her straight in the eye, "I guess it's just the two of us."

She was floored, stunned. "I—I can't go."

He dropped his gaze, shifted his weight, looked up again. "You're expected to go," he told her evenly. "Everyone is expected to go. It's important. It's...policy."

She stared at him. He stared at her, then he sighed. "Look, Cori, after all the business we've given you, it'll look bad if you don't attend. And it'll be a fun time, I guarantee it." He let that sink in, then he said, "I want you to be there. I really do. Come on your own if you like, but come. Please."

She sat there with the card in her hand, knowing she shouldn't go, a dozen different excuses in mind. Then suddenly she just tossed it all aside and got up. "Okay."

He shot her a grin over the top of his cola bottle. "Okay."

She nodded. "See you there." She turned and moved quickly toward the door, feeling herself smile, a little desperate to get away before he had her laughing and talking again.

"How many?" he called out.

She turned as she walked but kept moving. "Geneva doesn't like the beach."

He held up two fingers then in silent question. She nodded, her hand finding the doorknob. He got up off the desk, smiling, and rocked back gently on his heels. She opened the door and walked out, feeling wicked and jaunty and a little afraid all at the same time.

But it was only a picnic, she reasoned. A company picnic. There would be hundreds in attendance, and she needn't stay longer than she deemed wise. Dolly would love it. If Jerry were here, he would have to go, too. Guilt was not called for. It was one afternoon out of her life. She knew several others who would doubtlessly be there. And for Pete's sake, it was right in her own backyard.

She ought to go. She had to go. Reese wanted her to go—and after all her good resolutions and all her clever plans, that was all that really mattered.

Chapter Six

The morning was as clear and bright as glass, and though the breeze was crisp, it barely stirred the sultry air. Cori wore a pair of tight-fitting white jeans and a soft, pale blue shirt tied at the waist over a simple white maillot.

Dolly was as excited as Cori had ever seen her, her full bow of a mouth curved constantly into a smile, her jewel eyes sparkling. She stood impatiently and fidgeted while Cori brushed her glossy hair into a ponytail. Cori kissed her impulsively, and received a stout hug as reward. Dolly, too, wore her swimsuit beneath her clothing—a melon-colored, zippered jumpsuit, the legs of which they rolled to midcalf. In addition she wore canvas deck shoes without socks and toted a red-and-white-striped beach bag much too large for her.

Leaving Geneva with the affable Mrs. Campbell, they set out about ten o'clock in Cori's car, and half an hour later, after two wrong turns, reached the secluded picnic site. It looked as if all of Houston had beat them there.

Cars were parked helter-skelter along the sandy road; and a little farther on, two young men in jams and unbuttoned shirts were directing traffic into a designated parking area overgrown with marsh grasses and other tenacious vegetation. The beach was just beyond, but they had to hike through the overgrowth to get there, and in the process Cori lost a shoe, ripped right off her foot by a spike of the long, yellow grass. She felt as if she'd been scratched from head to toe by the time she got it back on her foot. Finally they emerged onto the pebbly sand.

People were everywhere—whole families staking out patches of warm sand with blankets, towels, chairs, umbrellas, radios, coolers, shoes, everything that came to hand. Children were running in the shallow surf. Adults were gathered in groups, cool drinks in their hands, laughter ringing out. Someone called her name, and Cori turned to find Evelyn Maybank, Reese's secretary, coming toward her. In jeans rolled to the knees and bare feet, Evelyn looked very different from her usual slightly dowdy self. Her brown hair was covered with a scarf, and in the sunlight her slightly ruddy skin looked fresh and clean.

Evelyn greeted them warmly and took time to make adoring sounds over Dolly and the usual comment about how very much she favored her aunt before pointing out the snack and drink tables erected some distance away beneath canopies of white canvas. They walked that way together, meeting Evelyn's husband and teenage son along the way. Cori saw others she knew, too: the Larks, in whose home she had dined with Jerry, and a number of engineers, including Carlton Cross, who carried a diapered toddler on his hip.

"I didn't know you had a little girl!" he said, stopping to admire a beaming Dolly.

Hoisting the beach bag over her shoulder, Cori introduced them and met young Mark, Carlton's nineteen-month-old son. Dolly loved the baby, though he threw sand in her eyes and pulled at her hair and lip. Carlton admonished him gently, but Dolly hugged him. Carlton went off with a reluctant Mark in tow to find his wife, and the trio of females went on to the food station.

She saw Reese at once, standing with his back to a slender pole at the corner of the canopy, a bottled soda in hand. He wore khaki swim trunks much like running shorts, a plain polo shirt of a similar shade and a thin white cardigan tossed over his shoulders, the sleeves looped loosely about his neck. He seemed to be staring out to sea, though it was impossible to tell for certain because of the dark glasses he wore, aviator style, she noticed, with narrow gold rims and reflective lenses. Evelyn called out to him, and his tanned face turned in the direction from which her voice came. Immediately he set aside his soft drink and started forward, trudging through the sand in his leather Top-siders already dark in places where they'd been splashed with water.

"My two favorite neighbors! Or should I say, my favorite consultant and her charming niece?"

"Either will do," she told him, thoroughly glad that she had come.

Evelyn excused herself and departed, saying she'd spotted an old friend. She went off, however, quite on her own. It occurred to Cori that she'd been delivered, much as if she'd been an important package, the arrival of which had been keenly anticipated. She turned a mildly suspicious eye on Reese, who reddened noticeably and cleared his throat.

"Can I, um, get you anything? There are sandwiches and snacks, if you're hungry. Tea, soft drinks, fruit juices..."

She shook her head to every suggestion. "We fortified ourselves with an enormous breakfast. Maybe later."

"Well, then," he said, turning Dolly away from the open tent and toward the beach, "there's a big ocean waiting to be played in, tons of sand to be fashioned into castles. We'll have a contest later to see who can make the best sand sculpture. I bet that'll be you and I. What d'you say?"

Dolly nodded her dark head enthusiastically, and with a secretive smile Corinne thought to herself that fate seemed bound and determined to make them a trio. The implications were sweet to ponder, and though Jerry and the attending difficulties came instantly to mind, she refused, for this one day, to let them spoil her fun.

"I just happen to have a spade and pail in here," she stated happily, bringing around the bag and letting it drop to the sand. Dolly began to loosen the drawstring excitedly.

"It's a red pail," she told Reese, "and it has a sifter!"

"Great!" The two of them went racing toward the water, spade and pail in hand. Cori laughed and tossed a large beach towel over her shoulder before gathering up the bag and following.

Dolly and Reese staked out a spot with an umbrella, stripped of nonessential clothing, and went to work, constructing a fanciful castle complete with excavated dungeon and moat. Cori watched for the most part, sitting cross-legged upon her towel beneath the umbrella and dispensing sun block and advice as needed. She noticed with unbidden satisfaction how they interacted together, laughing and talking, Dolly's dark head and his much lighter one bent over their project, each pair of hands complementing the other as they scooped and patted and stroked. She noticed, too, the bunch and ripple of firm muscle beneath tanned skin, the light sprinkling of sun-bleached hair over chest, forearms and shins, the crescent of a birthmark no bigger than the tip of her thumb upon his right calf. He was beautifully made, strong and healthy and masculine, all angles and planes and rolling hillocks. She thought of Jerry and how she once had marveled at his young body, and she knew he would be beautiful still and yet no match for the rugged example of unconscious male beauty before her. She was embarrassed yet thrilled by the feelings and thoughts that the sight of Reese aroused in her, and she learned quickly to be thankful for the distractions that presented themselves, the reeling cry of sea-birds, the leaping of fish and the occasional porpoise against the horizon, the antics of the surfers and bathers.

Most distracting of all were the people who frequently stopped by to say hello to the boss and admire his handiwork. Reese seemed perfectly at ease receiving them from his knees in the sand, clad only in swim trunks. He introduced his companions simply as Corinne and Dolly, no explanations, no surnames and no encouragement to ask questions. Nearly everyone seemed to understand tacitly that even the usual polite inquiries would be construed somehow as a breach of the good manners such interest was designed to display. However, one hapless employee did make so bold as to compliment Reese—and by implication Cori—on his taste in "friends" and was cut dead with a look designed to bring blood if not heart failure. The poor fellow quickly stammered a farewell and stumbled off, but he had succeeded in bringing a pall to the immediate atmosphere.

Cori stared out to sea, pondering the fact that she was allowing Reese to put himself in a compromising position, as well as jeopardizing Jerry's reputation and her own; and yet she could not make herself devise an excuse for parting company with him. As she wrestled with this, she felt herself pelted with sand and turned to find two wickedly grinning protagonists standing before her. Covered in grit from head to toe, they announced their creation complete and parted to show it off. She oohed and aahed as required, the difficulties of the situation shrinking in comparison to its obvious joys as she carefully inspected every square inch of the patently incongruous structure. The castle displayed both the precision and skill of the trained engineer and the fanciful sloppiness of a little girl's imagination. She pronounced it wonderful, as, indeed, it was, and succumbed immediately to their invitation to accompany them into the water and help them rinse the sand from their bodies and clothing.

They waited as she stood and peeled away her shirt, sandals and jeans, but it was Reese's gaze she felt upon her. A glance in his direction confirmed that he watched avidly, his face expressionless except for the frank appreciation in those pale blue eyes. A surge of pride caused her to draw up straight, presenting herself without action or word for his perusal. His gaze roamed boldly down and up, coming to rest without apology upon her face. She felt satisfaction spreading through her. He reached for her hand, and she delivered it into his without hesitation or compunction. He tugged her forward with a jerking motion that made Dolly squeal and run for the water, withdrawing for the moment in the ebb of a wave. They chased her into its receding edge, caught up and lifted her clear as the water rolled back in to shore.

The coldness made them gasp, but they waded on, Dolly bobbing between them, until the ends of Cori's hair floated upon the water and their bodies grew accustomed to the ocean chill. They turned back, trying to hold their places against the ebb and flow while Dolly clutched at them nervously, realizing how far from shore they were. Reese chided her gently.

"I thought you'd learned to swim."

"I did!" she protested.

"It's a little different from a swimming pool, isn't it?" he said calmly. "Why don't we practice? Cori and I will bridge our arms beneath you so you can't sink too far. Nothing to fear now. We'll hold you up. Ready? Kick those legs."

They linked both arms, holding each other just above the elbows. Cori wondered if her own skin was as warm to the touch as his was, then forgot about it as Dolly floundered and splashed between them. They had to literally hold her up at first, but gradually she relaxed, and gained her equilibrium. Slowly, with a little coaching, her floundering became long, even strokes, and finally she was kicking with hardly a splash. She began to move away from them, and suddenly a wave rolled in, propelling her along with it. Panicked, Cori started after her, but Reese caught her about the waist and pulled her back. Her heart in her throat, the water buffeting her against him, she watched as the wave crested beneath the child and gently dissipated, leaving her stroking along in water so shallow that she quickly found her feet and simply stood up.

Dolly turned, waving wildly. Relief, pride and gratitude flooded through Cori, receding in the wake of a sudden awareness of the arm about her waist, the leg against hers, the chafing of the hem of his trunks against her thigh, her shoulder knocking into his ribs. She turned her head to find Reese looking, not at Dolly, but at *her*. Instantly her heart pounded. Ocean, earth and sky were forgotten, blocked out by the mental sensation of the imagined fulfillment of desire. She felt herself turn, fit her body fully to his, lift her arms about his neck....

"Here I come!"

The cry brought reality back into sharp focus. At her side, Reese turned his gaze forward. His arm released her, and their bodies drifted apart. He moved away, and she felt a sudden, sharp sense of loss.

"Better meet her."

She nodded and followed, trying not to think what she was thinking, what she was wanting, knowing it was hopeless. Dolly struggled toward them, and Cori concentrated on her, steeling herself against her own feelings when Reese got to the child first, caught her in his arms, lifted her and turned her back toward shore. She heard his words of praise, his firm caution against swimming out on her own, and Dolly's excited chatter as she poised for a second demonstration of her skill.

When Cori reached shore, they were spreading their towels over the sand and collapsing upon them. She joined them, adding her laughter to theirs, making the easy small talk of chums as if every nerve in her body was not straining for the feel or sense of Reese. After a while, they dried off enough to put their clothes back on over their damp suits. Dolly declared herself hungry, and Cori seized the need to escort her to the snack bar as a means by which to put distance between herself, her fantasies and Reese, only to have him declare his own middle empty and accompany them.

Temporarily abandoning castle, umbrella, bag and towels, they went in search of sustenance. Minutes later, laden with fruit, sandwiches and cold drinks, they settled at a table beneath the great white awning. To her surprise, Cori discovered her appetite had awakened, and she munched her way through a chicken sandwich, a banana and a chocolate-chip cookie while Dolly worked on a single apple, abandoning it the moment a pair of teenage girls trotted past the station on shaggy horses. Seeing her obvious interest, Reese suggested they stroll over toward the rental concessions. Long before they reached the corral where the vendor kept his mounts, however, they could see that it was empty. Dolly looked up with solemn disappointment and cheerful resignation coupled in her clear green eyes, and Reese went down on one knee.

"Tell you what," he said, "if you'll just be patient, I'll see to it you get to ride, and it won't be on some woolly old nag but on a real horse fit for a princess. What do you say? Can you wait a few days?"

"A real princess's horse?" Dolly asked breathlessly.

"Um-hmm. In fact, her name is Lady Royale, and she's all gold and white."

"Oh, she sounds wonderful."

"She is," he assured her. "She belongs to a very good friend of mine, and if you'll just be patient, I'll have her brought over to the house soon, and we'll all go riding."

Dolly threw her arms about his neck then, forestalling any protest Cori might have made about inconvenience and lack of experience. He chuckled, then suddenly she bolted away, running back down the beach in the direction from which they'd come. Cori turned to follow and spotted Carlton Cross and young Mark leading a group of children toward them. Dolly joined them, hopping about and exclaiming garbled news about a royal horse, all gold, coming for a ride to Reese's house. Reese stood, his laughter mingling with Cori's as the party drew near.

"Can Dolly come with us?" Carlton asked. She was on her knees goo-gooing to the baby, the other kids alternately snickering and trying to outdo her. "We're going hunting for treasure."

Dolly looked up then, pleading in her eyes. "Sure," Cori told them, and the whole group moved off. "Be careful," she called after them. "Stay together!" Carlton lifted a hand in acknowledgement.

"Yes, Mother," he called.

"She's my auntie," Dolly corrected, but the rest of their words were lost on a breeze that whipped in from the ocean, ruffling hair and swirling the clumps of grass.

Reese moved at her side, blocking the little group from view, and it occurred to Cori that the trio was now a duet. Or perhaps a couple? Something told her the same thought had occurred to him.

"What now?" he asked, as if confirming her suspicion. "You up for a game of volleyball?"

She grinned at him, seizing the diversion he offered her. "Is that a challenge?"

"And what if it is?" he goaded.

"Then I'd have to accept, of course."

"Foolish woman," he said, and moved off at a trot, speeding up when she fell in beside him, so that they raced to see who could get to the volleyball net first.

He beat her, but just barely, and she'd pressed him hard enough that they both had to stop and catch their breath before they could shed their shoes and join in the game in progress. They played several games, first on opposite teams, then on the same side. He was, of course, much more proficient than she, but this was all fun and little competition, with more clowning going on than real playing. The Top Gun drew a good bit of banter and teasing, but it was all good-natured and in the spirit of clean fun.

Finally Cori had to fall out, exhausted from all the cavorting in deep sand beneath a sun that shone down hotter than she'd realized. Reese joined her, panting, head bowed over bent knees. After a rest, he suggested a cool drink, and she was only too glad to agree. They got up and trudged toward the drink bar, where they commandeered a couple of sodas before wandering down to shake the sand out of the towels and spread them in the shade of their umbrella.

Content to rest and slake their thirst, they leaned back on their elbows and watched the waves roll in, silent, companionable, at ease. Cori was close to dozing when Evelyn joined them, her hair flying about in the breeze.

"It's about that time, Top," she informed Reese. He grumbled and sat up, turning his face toward the setting sun.

"Okay. Start calling them in. Have a few of the guys gather wood for the fires. You checked with the caterer?"

She nodded. "Barbecue's hot. Salad's cold. Potatoes are bursting their skins. They're throwing on the shrimp now."

"Have you seen Carlton and the kids?" Cori asked, forcing herself into a sitting position.

"Nope. Somebody said they went off toward the jetty."

Cori frowned. "Where's that?"

"Never mind," Reese interjected, rising to stand and offering Cori a helping hand. "We'll walk down that way and see if we can spot them. Evelyn, my darling, you start herding the company cattle toward the feed troughs, and remind me Monday morning to give you a raise."

She smiled broadly. "Yes, sir!" She bounced up and hurried away while Cori was still getting her own feet beneath her.

"Don't know what I'd do without her," he said, watching the other woman go. Then, suddenly, he was looking into Cori's eyes, his hand settling in the small of her back. "Don't know when I've enjoyed a day more." And that pale blue gaze said it wasn't all Evelyn's doing.

She wanted very much to go on tiptoe and bring her mouth against his, but she didn't dare, and so she smiled and turned away, willing her heart to abandon its powerful hammering and beat a sedate staccato. He steered her down the beach. A few people called out to them, and they hailed a few others to ask if they'd seen Carlton and his crew of kids.

"Toward the jetty" was the collective consensus, and they walked on, rounding the gentle point where the sea-wall began, until they found themselves alone with the call of the birds and the rush of the waves, the scene of the picnic hidden from view by the curve of the land and the spikes of marsh grass.

"There," he said, pointing toward a line of gray, broken rock jutting out to sea. But there was no sign of the children. They picked up their pace, reaching the jetty in the space of a minute or two. Perhaps ten feet high, with sloping sides and a flat top, it resembled nothing more than a rough rectangle of piled stones and chunks of concrete. "They must have climbed over," he said, eying the rough structure. "Guess we'd better do the same."

She didn't like the look of that pile of rock, but she liked even less the idea of Dolly and the other children clambering over it. Carlton should have had better sense, she mused. But she was also thinking that if they could do it, so could she. Reese took her hand and started up, choosing his footholds carefully. She climbed after him, her first step uncertain, the next one even more so as the rock she'd chosen shifted beneath her foot.

"Oh!" She felt herself slip backward, the strap of her sandal snapping, but even as she fell, Reese came after her, his hand tightening around hers. Her bare foot found the sand, and his arm came around her at the same instant. They stumbled, but he caught her to him and held her there. Suddenly she was looking up into his eyes, seeing much there to give her pause and more to light fires and melt even the most icy resistance. She saw the same deci-

sive resolve in the set of his jaw and the line of his mouth
and knew, finally, that it couldn't be stopped. Some place,
some time, it must inevitably come to this. Why not here?
Why not now? His answer was his hand at the back of her
head and his mouth seizing hers.

She clung to him and gave herself up to her fate will-
ingly, joyfully, her body reacting in myriad ways. She was
hungry for him and parted her lips, taking his tongue deep
into her mouth, feeling the rush of his breath against her
cheek and in the hard expansion of his chest against her
breasts. Giving as good as she got, she pressed her body to
his, her hands invading his hair and exploring the tight
bunch and roll of his shoulders and back and hips. It
wasn't enough for either of them.

His hands roamed in fits and starts, and his mouth left
hers to travel the column of her throat. She arched against
him, gasping as her skin prickled and hot chills washed
through her. His mouth came back again to take hers and
plunder it, fierce in its possession, ruthless. They were
starving souls, gobbling in the midst of sudden bounty,
feeding on one another, until desire threatened to break the
bonds and make them a single entity, glutted with sensation and greedy for more.

He pulled the blouse from her shoulders and ran his
hands over her skin. She responded with fingers that
pushed up beneath his shirt, lifting it to expose the broad,
hard plains of his torso. He found the strap of her suit and
peeled it back, his hand dropping to the swollen mound of
her breasts, shielded still by the clinging, elastic fabric, but
not for long. His breath hissed into the cavern of her
mouth as his hand swept the barrier away, found the flesh
it sought and closed around it. She convulsed against him,
her head falling back as his mouth slid downward. She felt
herself sagging beneath the weight of mutual desire, felt his

arms pulling her down, sensed the cool sand coming up to meet her.... Suddenly the sound of a child's voice reached them, its taunt ringing sharp and clear.

"You can't catch me! You can't catch me!"

They fell apart, split by the sudden rush of reality, and in the same instant he reached out for her, shielding her with his arms and body. It was a moment before they realized that they were still alone, that the children's voices came to them from the other side of the ten-foot-high rock jetty. Gasping with relief, Cori pulled the shirt up onto her shoulders, lifted the strap into place beneath it and smoothed the fabric over her breast, but even as she did this, the color began to rise in her cheeks. Reese hugged her close, tightening his embrace again and again as the sounds of children walking and running together came ever closer. They heard the first one reach the opposite side of the jetty.

"I won! I won!"

"Don't go up till the captain gets there," another warned. "He'll have you walk the plank!"

The first called such silly threats baby-talk, and they began to argue. It was then that he released her, his arms loosening and slowly falling away. Reluctantly she moved from the solid comfort of his chest. He lifted a hand and forced her gaze up with a finger curled beneath her chin. His eyes met hers boldly.

"I should be sorry," he said softly. "I'm not. I don't want you to be."

"No one has to be sorry," she told him, taking his hand. "You see, it doesn't have to be—"

"Captain Cross, sir," a childish voice called out. "Permission to climb this mountain!"

"Hold on there, matey, till the crew's in position." It was Carlton's voice, just the other side of the jetty, but she didn't want the moment to slip away too soon. Reese needed to know the truth; she needed to tell him. She opened her mouth.

"Cap'n Cross," Dolly's little voice said, "can I hold Marky's hand this time?"

"We'll both hold his hands," Carlton replied. "Up you go now."

Reese looked at her hand, then turned his face toward the rock wall of the jetty. Too late. The moment had passed. Reese called out, "Hey there, you pirates, need any help?"

"Ho! It's the admiral," Carlton said. "We could use a hand with the treasure."

Reese gave her fingers a final squeeze and let go, stepping up onto the lowest outcropping of rock. He climbed swiftly and easily and was on the top before the first of them. He gave a boy of about ten a hand up and another down, and repeated the procedure with the next child. Meanwhile, Cori found her broken shoe and quickly shed the other one in time to move out of the way as the boy hopped down onto the sand.

"I'm gonna beat!" he called, running off toward the picnic site, but Cori reasoned that it would be a hollow victory without competition, as no one else seemed interested in catching up with him.

She dropped her shoes and helped the second child down, and then a third and a fourth and so on, until Carlton himself handed down young Mark, wet from the waist down and not, Cori suspected from mere seawater. At the very end came Dolly, babbling happily about the shells they'd found and the games they'd played, and Carlton and Reese, who toted a damp, sandy paper bag clinking with discovered treasure.

Carlton took Mark and set him on his feet, apologizing to Cori for the boy's condition as he withdrew a packet of disinfecting wipes from his back pocket. He passed them out among crew and interlopers alike, dismissing each to frolic down the beach toward parents and dinner, until only he, his son, Reese, Dolly and Cori were left. Together, the five of them set off at a leisurely pace that young Mark could manage without being carried. Dolly and Carlton chatted excitedly about their adventures, Dolly from her place between Reese and Cori, her little hands holding on to theirs. No one seemed to notice that Reese and Cori remained silent.

Corinne herself was quite recovered by the time they rejoined the picnic. All that had happened between them could only be right and natural, as far as she was concerned. She had felt it from their first meeting—this attraction that would not go away—and now she had solid proof that he had been feeling it, too. Her embarrassment had stemmed only from the thought of being caught making love, with this man of all men, on a public beach. But that hadn't happened, and now that the possibility of it was behind her, she saw no need to give it further thought and turned her mind to other matters.

The next logical step was to tell Reese the truth about Jerry. But how to do it best? She was both sad and glad that she hadn't blurted it out back there, sad because it could all be out now, glad because she hadn't hurt Jerry by the telling and could now decide how best to handle it for his sake. She truly didn't want to hurt Jerry. In fact, she was beginning to feel a renewed sense of gratitude to him for bringing her here. Had she not come, she would never have met Reese Compton and . . . fallen in love?

She turned impulsively to look at him standing behind her at the end of the buffet line. Their eyes met and held, and she felt his hand brush against her wrist, almost as if he couldn't keep his hands off her an instant longer, and in that moment she knew she was in love. Someone called out to him, and his gaze turned away, but the look and the touch stayed with her, infusing her with a warmth and an energy she had never before experienced. Never. Not even as a starry-eyed eighteen-year-old graced with the attentions of the current campus version of Adonis, and she had truly thought herself in love then, then and since—until now, until Reese. She had only to bide her time and trust that her feelings were returned.

It was some time before the first doubt darkened her euphoria. Perhaps it started when Reese excused himself from her side and his dinner to go and talk with a beckoning friend, or when they called on him to make a speech and he took his place in front of the salad bar, as calm and collected as she'd ever seen him. The ease with which he addressed the gathering amazed her. He was the man behind the desk again, the one they talked about at dinner parties and wrote up on the front pages of national newspapers. She began to remember things they'd said of him—that celebrated sense of honor, the conservative outlook, the old-fashioned personal code.

"I should be sorry," he'd said, and suddenly she was thinking of that statement in a new way. Would he be sorry about what they'd done? Was he sorry already? If so, how long before he came to despise her? Not that she would ever know for certain. He would take the majority of the blame himself and play the part of the gentleman to the very end—cool, superior, more and more distant as time went on.

She had to tell him the truth, quickly, before the feeling between them washed away in a flood of guilt. He would understand once she explained why she'd gone along with the deception. Wouldn't he? Or would he see only the lie? And what would that mean for Jerry? Would he lose the respect of his boss, or would he lose his job? She thought of Geneva, too, and of the confusion she would inevitably feel. Suddenly it didn't seem so simple anymore. Suddenly it was no longer a matter of wait and trust, but of wait and hope. Wait and hope—and pray.

Chapter Seven

Reese Compton was a man who kept his promises, a man with a gift for making tough, complex decisions; and yet he literally agonized over keeping his promise to Dolly. He regretted even mentioning to the child the possibility of a horseback ride, and at the same time delighted in having a legitimate reason for spending time with Corinne. It did not help his state of mind to know that he alone was responsible for his agony.

He had manipulated the events of the previous Saturday with cold-blooded dedication to his own interests, beginning with the decision to reactivate a long-abandoned practice of including independent contractors in the annual company picnic. He had followed that by hand-delivering Corinne's invitation in surroundings and circumstances carefully chosen to intimidate and thereby prevent a refusal. After that, it was merely a matter of assigning a few trusted subordinates to keep an eye out for her arrival at the beach and deliver her to him. The rest he'd managed all on his own—and had had a damned good time doing it. Only the kiss had he failed to plan.

Losing his head was not something to which Reese Compton was accustomed. Even now he didn't know how it had happened. One moment they were climbing the broken, rocky slope of the jetty, and the next he was making love to her. He possessed no illusions about how it would have turned out if Carlton hadn't come along with the children when he had, at least as far as his own intentions. He couldn't say with any confidence what Corinne would have done or allowed. She had not been an unwilling participant, but to what point would she have continued to be so? Moreover, he could not be certain what her feelings toward him were now. Her initial reaction upon the realization of what they were doing had seemed to be shame, and that had hurt him, wounded him deeply. Yet what else could he reasonably expect? The woman was engaged to another man, *in love* with another man.

No. He could not accept the idea that Corinne loved Jerry Arnold. No woman in love with one man could have responded as she had with another. Everything in him said that Corinne's engagement to Jerry was a mistake, a fluke. Maybe it had been a hasty decision for both of them, fueled by memories of a past relationship. No one knew better than Reese what memories could do to a person. But the fact remained that Cori was engaged to Jerry. Given that fact, she might be ashamed of how she'd handled that situation at the jetty. It stood to reason that if she was ashamed of her own behavior, she would be appalled at his. Having witnessed her emotional struggle that evening, he could only wonder what her feelings were at the moment. She had seemed to vacillate from one extreme to another, smiling one minute, frowning the next—and he had been totally incapable of influencing or comforting her, given the very public circumstances.

He would have liked to believe that if he could have taken her in his arms once more and declared what he himself was feeling, she would have revealed similar sentiments, Jerry Arnold or no Jerry Arnold; yet he knew this hope was vain, even dishonorable, and he could not cavalierly allow himself to pursue it, for her sake any more than his own. How could he allow her to soil her conscience? On the other hand, if by some miracle she felt about him as he did about her, was it right to deny that genuine feeling and in the process, perhaps, see her marry a man he was almost certain she didn't love?

His thoughts were interrupted when Evelyn buzzed to say that the executive committee had arrived to discuss their London options. He ran a hand over his face, exhaling in self-disgust, then steeled himself with a deep breath before signaling his permission to enter. They filed in, three division heads and their vice presidents, Mort Hardesty, his own designated second-in-command, and Evelyn herself, who would take notes of the meeting. He greeted each with a stiff smile and allowed them some moments to arrange themselves in chairs about the room. He did not get up, and he didn't mince words.

"Ladies and gentlemen, I want names, anyone and everyone you think appropriate to handle the London chair. Mort, we'll begin with you."

Mort, who happened to be several years Reese's senior and about as big as a chipmunk, folded his arms. "Jerry Arnold," he said, "if we can wait until he finishes in Brazil."

"But can we?" someone else put in.

"Or do we pull him out of South America now?"

"Mike McCutcheon could probably handle it," a new voice proposed.

"Handle what?" came the question. "London or Brazil?"

Reese scowled and let them ramble on. Normally, he would have directed the conversation himself, extracting a list of names and then discussing each in turn. That Jerry's name had been the first mentioned neither surprised nor unsettled him, but it didn't make the decision any easier, either, for reasons to which only he was privy—he hoped. The truth was that he'd like nothing better than to have Jerry Arnold disappear off the face of the earth, but that wasn't an option; London was. It was also a promotion, a big one, but he had no doubt that Jerry Arnold could handle it. In fact, despite the other names being bandied about, Jerry was probably the man for the job. Still, there were other considerations.

Would Cori like London? he wondered angrily. Or would she prefer to stay closer to her beloved niece? She was going to miss that child terribly. Nothing had been said yet about Dolly going home, but eventually she must, of course, presumably before the new school year started. Jerry ought to be back from Brazil by then, and he would want to be married right away, no doubt—unless he'd already been sent to London. But did he, Reese, dare take such a step, knowing Cori might refuse to go with Jerry, or did he refuse the opportunity to Jerry on that account? What was the right thing to do? Was there a right course available to him anymore?

God, what a mess! He groaned inwardly, swatting at an ink pen that lay on his desk pad. The pen clattered noisily to the floor, producing instant silence. His hand came up, a wry, practiced smile twisting his mouth. He cleared his throat.

"Excuse me. Where were we?"

He let them go on for another quarter of an hour before dismissing the whole lot, no closer to a decision than before and utterly helpless to provoke one. He templed his fingers and bowed his head over them, thinking, thinking, until it felt as if his skull would explode with the effort. At last, the grim set of his features reflecting his choice, he picked up the telephone receiver and dialed the familiar number. Corinne herself answered the phone. He felt his expression soften into a smile.

"Anybody there want to take a ride this afternoon?" he asked, and the sound of her laughter soothed his remaining doubts. He settled back into his chair, his mood lifting significantly as she gave him the answer. He told himself he shouldn't be so pleased, shouldn't feel so damned smug; but what option did he have except to play this thing out to some sort of conclusion?

"How's three o'clock?" he heard himself say, marveling at his calmness. "Good. I'll see the two of you then." A moment later he hung up and pivoted his chair to one side, rubbing his chin thoughtfully.

Well, she hadn't turned him down. That ought to mean something, if he just knew what. But there was no use in thinking about it now. He abruptly hit the call button on the intercom.

"Evelyn, I'm leaving early. Do me a favor and call the Waltons. Tell them I want to borrow a rig and two horses, Lady Royale and..." He considered briefly. No use taking a chance. He wanted Corinne on a mount he knew she could handle. "The Parson," he decided, recalling the placid gelding. She'd sit better on Son of Night, his own big black, but with a mare and an inexperienced rider around, it wouldn't be prudent. Not that prudence was the order of the day. He'd abandoned real prudence with that kiss on the beach—probably even before. But there wasn't time for second-guessing. He had a date with two compelling ladies—and he meant to keep it. God help him.

He left the office within the hour, but not by the usual means of private elevator to the helicopter pad on the roof of the building. This time he went down and walked out the front door, remembering ruefully that the last occasion on which he had done so, he had been in the company of Jerry Arnold. A car and driver were waiting for him. He gave the man directions to the Waltons' ranch near the city of Alvin, and as they were driving, shed his coat and tie and rolled up his shirtsleeves. That done, he settled back to wait, but a glance at his watch told him he had cut it awfully close. There would be no time for chatting with his old friends, and he would have to be sure to make it up to them at a later time. He'd done this kind of thing before, borrowing mounts on short notice, but he feared his choice of the plodding Parson would elicit questions he'd rather not answer.

He needn't have worried. Neither of the senior Watsons were at home. Their daughter, who had assumed much of the responsibility for the day-to-day operation of the ranch and stables, had the rig waiting and loaded with the two horses he had specified. She asked no questions, saying only that he should return the vehicle, trailer and animals at his convenience. Much relieved, he sent his driver and car back to Houston, climbed behind the wheel of the Waltons' rusty old pickup truck, and headed for the island.

By three, he'd reached his own small stable, unloaded the two animals into stalls flanking that of Son of Night, given them each a scoop of sweetfeed, and was sliding into a pair of jeans when the doorbell rang. He raced to the door in his stocking feet, shoving his arms into shirt-sleeve, and greeted a smiling Cori and a positively electric Dolly.

"Oh boy!" the child gushed. "We're going riding! Is she here? Is she here? Is the princess horse here?"

"Let me get my boots," he exclaimed, laughing, "and I'll take you to meet her!"

"She's been like this ever since you called," Cori told him apologetically. "I could hardly get her dressed, she was hopping around so."

He gave them each a perusal at that and nodded, seeing they both wore jeans and lightweight shirts with long sleeves to protect against sunburn. Cori had on a pair of half boots with square toes and flat heels, while Dolly wore sneakers with two pairs of thick socks turned down over her ankles.

"Be with you in a minute," he said, hurrying back to his bedroom. It occurred to him that neither of them had ever been in his house before, and he called out that they should look around and make themselves at home, not that there was much to look at, really. People were almost invariably disappointed in the house, but he didn't usually mind. It was his home, after all, and he'd had it built to please himself, with one enormous room running through its center.

This all-purpose great room had soaring walls that culminated in a cathedral ceiling overhead, a large rock fireplace that faced onto a living room setting of brightly colored couches and chairs strewn with an abundance of pillows, a state-of-the-art stereo system, display cases filled with an amazing variety of collectible art pieces, large and colorful Navajo rugs, and tables of every size, shape, function and wood. Off this great hall were two separate wings—one consisting of two very large and well-appointed bedrooms, complete with sitting areas, hot tubs, and private patios, the other comprising a small, efficient kitchen, an enviable wine cellar, a little-used dining room and extraordinary storage spaces.

It was his home, his haven, designed to allow him to entertain, but very much a bachelor's house. Perhaps by building it as he had, he'd insulated himself from the possibility of remarriage and family. Without doubt, he would have chosen to live very differently if Gayla and Kenneth still shared his life.

What, he wondered wryly, pulling on the first boot, had him thinking along these lines now? *As if you don't know,* he chided himself, stomping his foot into place. He reached for the second boot, wanting to believe his fantasies hadn't gone so far that he was actually beginning to think of marriage again.

When he returned to Corinne and Dolly, they were chatting quietly before a cabinet of curios. "I like the yellow one with the splotches," Cori commented, and Dolly giggled.

"It looks like a paint pot that somebody mixed too many colors of paint in."

"Don't be silly," Cori admonished gently. "I'm sure it's quite valuable."

"Actually, it isn't," Reese told her, and they both turned to face him. "It's merely interesting. Every valuable piece I've ever collected has been donated to a museum somewhere. I don't believe in individuals hoarding artifacts. They need to be studied, appreciated and owned by everyone. I keep only those things that have some special significance for me. You were right, by the way, Dolly. That little paint pot was owned and used by a rather obscure primitive artist in Louisiana. She was a remarkable woman, the granddaughter of slaves, with a third-grade education, who painted on fabric canvases she bleached and stretched herself. She once painted my son into a New Orleans street scene, and though she wouldn't allow me to buy the painting, she gave me the paint pot.''

In his mind's eye, he pictured that scene: little Kenny, barely toddling, clutching the rail of a rusty cast-iron fence and gazing with fascination at the face of a black girl, perhaps eight years old, who entertained him with a wagging tongue, while the street bustled with eyeless adults consumed by their own selfish interests. He had been astonished at the rapidity with which the artist had worked. The little boy hadn't truly been recognizable as Kenny. The woman's talent had not been portraiture. Yet the composition and imagery were incredibly strong. That single experience had bound him with that artist for the remainder of her life. He had followed her career avidly, more avidly than she. The painting now hung in a New York gallery on permanent display. He could not bear to look at it, but somehow the paint pot continued to bring to him that feeling of astonishment blended with pride and understanding. He took a deep breath, hearing Corinne's soft voice.

"I didn't know you have a son."

"I don't."

The reply had been automatic and unintentionally harsh, but he couldn't bring himself to apologize or to explain. Instead, he softened his expression visibly and forced a cheerful tone into his voice.

"Who's ready to ride?"

Dolly grinned broadly, and he concentrated on her, taking her hand and hurrying her toward the back of the house. Corinne followed but in a subdued fashion, her head bowed, her hands gathering her hair at the nape of her neck. He led them out into the sunlight. They should all be wearing hats, but he was unwilling to delay long enough to rectify the oversight. The ride would have to be short. Perhaps that was best after all.

They crossed the sandy grounds without speaking, walking rapidly away from the house and toward the bayou. Unlike the owners of Jerry's residence, he had elected to build his home away from the bayou, removing the fear of occasional flooding and, therefore, the need for building atop inelegant stilts. What he missed by not having his boat docks right outside his back door was more than recompensed by the graceful, balanced, burgundy brick facade of his house and the perfect symmetry of its white roof.

The sweet, musty shade of the stable was always welcome to him but even more so on a warm, bright day. The three horses reacted with low sniggers as the three of them entered the little barn, pausing to allow their eyes time to adjust to the sudden lack of light. His own eyes adjusted more quickly than the others', and he left them to gather the tack, saddle and blankets for Lady Royale. The saddle was not exactly meant for a child, but it was dainty enough for the smallest woman, and its pale leather complemented the palomino's golden coat.

Dolly ran to aid him as he carried the gear toward the end stall where Lady Royale waited obediently, snorting a greeting as they drew near. He deposited both gear and child out of harm's way, but Dolly tried to compensate for distance and dimness by rising on tiptoe and craning her neck.

"She's big!" she noted, giggling nervously.

"But well behaved," he assured her, patting the horse's rump affectionately. He took the blanket from the pile at Dolly's feet and shook it out. The child coughed as dust flew. "Sorry about that," he said as he bent to sling the bridle over his shoulder. "I'm not used to short people. My own head's well above the dust."

"That's okay," she told him, sounding a little strangled. Cori had moved to the far stall, correctly picking out her own mount and getting acquainted in gentle tones that might have been more enthusiastic. Reese forgot the child's sniffles as he silently cursed himself for having mentioned Kenneth and bringing this pall on himself and Cori. Grimly, he moved to the horse and spread the blanket, then delivered the bit to the horse's mouth and pulled the bridle into place. When he went back for the saddle, he noticed that Dolly's eyes were wide and moist, but he absently attributed it to the dust he had thoughtlessly scattered, his senses much more attuned to the woman standing apart from them.

For several minutes, his attention was taken entirely by the business of settling the saddle, tightening the cinch and shortening the stirrups. He heard the small snufflings and gaspings, but they didn't really register, for above them he somehow heard the sound of Cori's voice and the snorted replies of the charmed gelding, accompanied by the impatient shuffles and blows of Son of Night, jealous at a lack of similar attention. It was only when Lady Royale herself began to shiver and dance away from his touch that he realized something was not right. Even as he soothed the normally sedate palomino with stroking hands, he sent his gaze around the area, spying Dolly only as she slumped to the ground.

"Dol-*ly!* Corinne!"

Lady Royale danced to one side, alarmed, momentarily penning him in the stall. He literally shoved her, both hands on her flinching hindquarter, and she moved, snorting her confusion. He reached the child just before Corinne, his gaze taking in her whitened face, wide eyes, mouth rimmed with a bluish stain. He watched her trembling body strain, heard the wheezing gasp and the painful rattle from deep in her chest as she tried frantically to work her lungs, and instantly he was standing over his son's bed, impotent with the awful knowledge that he was dying, one shallow breath at a time.

"Get her out of here!" Corinne's harsh edict snapped him back to the present, and he stooped to gather the small body in his arms. "Hurry!" she commanded, literally shoving him. He strode down the dark aisle and out into the paralyzing sunlight. "Get her to the house!" she shouted, closing the corral gates behind them. He moved quickly, mechanically, wishing with all his being that he was somewhere else, *anywhere* else. Corinne raced past him, veering toward the trees that separated his grounds from those of the Arnolds. "I'll get the atomizer. God, why didn't I think to bring it with me!"

He barely heard her as he concentrated on getting the child indoors. Once there, he suffered a moment of horrifying panic. Dolly was dead weight in his arms, gagging and wheezing, her eyes rolled back to expose whites ebbed with bloodshot red. He heard himself screaming but knew not what he said, to whom he spoke. *Help!* he thought. *I have to get help!* And in his mind's eye he saw himself rushing to the door, shouting for the nurse. When he bumped into the sofa, he automatically deposited the wheezing, unconscious child and lunged for the cordless phone hidden in a box upon the end table, covering her with his body. He rolled away, fearful that he might crush her and compound her problems. His hands ripped at the box, the receiver, the antennae. On his knees upon the floor, he punched in the emergency number, and an instant later blurted the address into the phone. Suddenly he became aware of an awful, deadly silence.

"She's not breathing! She's not breathing!" He was repeating it still when Corinne tore into the room, the phone lying discarded upon the rug.

What happened next was a blur to him, events remembered later in fleeting snatches. There was Cori compressing the child's chest with her forearms while fitting something into her mouth. It seemed to him at one point that she was beating the child, shaking her, and though it angered him, he could do nothing. Then, too, he saw Kenneth being flopped about like a rag doll upon the bed, saw the nurse pounding his little back with the flat of her fist. Others ran into the room, some of them nurses in white and technicians in long, blue coats and, in different surroundings that he recognized as his own home, uniformed attendants. He saw Dolly's face contorted by an oxygen mask, or was it Kenny's? No matter. It was one and the same, the pain indistinguishable from that he had already suffered. They were intimately acquainted, this pain and he.

He realized at one point that Cori was speaking rapidly, but though he heard the words, he didn't recognize them, and yet he nodded, made some sound of acknowledgment. It was only when she cupped his face with her hands that he felt grounded and aware, understood the urgency. That the two events were separated by time was a fact he sensed only vaguely, but he knew in some part of his mind that they had to go, and he moved with her, dreamlike, toward the door. It was in the glare of the sunshine that he came fully to himself, recognizing the threatening presence of the ambulance and its implication.

Numbly, he helped Cori into the back of the cramped van and climbed up after her. The attendant hovered over Dolly's slight form, so still now, and the driver closed them inside. As Cori groped for his hand, they lurched forward, sirens wailing. Working quickly and smoothly, the attendant unbuttoned Dolly's blouse and slipped one arm free of its sleeve. Next he opened a small red box and began to prepare an injection. A moment later he swiped at the exposed skin of her arm with an alcohol prep and plunged the needle in. Reese looked away. Somewhere between the house and the hospital, the child coughed, gagged and began to weep weakly, soliciting his gaze. Cori reached out for her, spreading her arms across her lower body, and put her head down on the edge of the gurney, sighing with relief.

"I think we're going to be all right," the attendant said in a calm, authoritative voice. But Reese knew differently. Children died every day in this world of modern medical miracles, some of them by inches, others in one shocking rush. It mattered not what route they took. Each led to a kind of devastation so utter and so bleak that no one ever fully recovered. He was living proof of that. Gayla had been another. It was a journey he had no intention of repeating. Ever.

The attendant settled the oxygen mask more comfortably on Dolly's face and stroked the dark hair from her forehead before reaching for a blanket. Cori helped him spread the blanket over the child, comforting her with pats and rubs. Almost immediately Dolly dropped off into exhausted sleep, completely unaware when the attendant slipped the cold stethoscope beneath the blanket. He listened, straight-faced, then removed the apparatus and took up a clipboard, bracing himself against the roll of the vehicle.

"Her name is Dolly Paris?" he asked mechanically, just rechecking the facts. Cori answered him, and he went on, rattling off birth date, current address, telephone number. "Has she ever experienced an episode of asthma before?"

"Yes, frequently."

"Any bronchitis?"

"Chronic."

"Allergies?"

"Undoubtedly."

"She ever been tested?"

Cori sighed. "No. I meant to have it done right away, but she's been so much better since we came here that I let it go. I could kick myself."

"Don't blame yourself," Reese told her, his voice deep and rough with the effort of speaking. "It's not really your responsibility." She glanced at him over her shoulder, her expression puzzled, but he was too tired, too emotionally spent to comprehend its meaning. The paramedic scribbled and went on with his questions.

"Is she insured?"

"There is some coverage." She struggled with company names and policy numbers.

Reese mentally withdrew, reemerging moments later when the attendant asked, "Which of you is the child's legal guardian?"

"Neither," Reese answered automatically.

"I am," Cori said at the same time.

He stared at her, sure he'd misunderstood, but those emerald eyes looked back at him implacably. "You're her aunt."

"And her legal guardian." He blinked, confused. She smirked grimly. "Jerry apparently left out that little detail. I thought you knew." He could only shake his head.

"If you'll just sign by the X," the attendant said, pushing the clipboard and a pen at her. Reluctantly, Cori turned her gaze away and took the pen in hand.

Reese put his head back and made himself breathe slowly, deeply and silently. He was alone, apart from the jostle of the ambulance, the wail of the siren, the indifferent professionalism of the attendant. Nothing more than observer now, he nevertheless closed his eyes, telling himself that Dolly belonged to Cori, and Cori belonged to Jerry Arnold. These were the facts, the undeniable facts. What had he been thinking? What had possessed him to consider challenging this basic tenet of their lives? He was safe alone, stronger alone. He couldn't lose what wasn't his to begin with. He was safe. Safe.

He seized the shield of honor and responsibility once more. She was Jerry's woman. They were Jerry's family. He'd promised to look after them, and Reese Compton was a man who kept his promises. He'd said nothing about love. Indeed, was he not honor bound to withhold his love? It was the decent thing to do. They were Jerry's to love; not his.

He'd been confused about that for a while. What did it matter why? There were reasons enough: it had been too long since he'd been with a woman. Dolly had reminded him of Kenny, bringing back unwanted memories. He hadn't understood all the rules, all the facts. It didn't matter. He wouldn't let it matter. Ever. He couldn't. He didn't dare.

Never again, he promised himself. Never again.

Chapter Eight

The room was full of roses. Corinne put her hand to her sleek hair and inhaled their rich fragrance, feeling guilty because she was not more pleased. The flowers had cost a small fortune, no doubt about it, yet she still thought of them as one of Jerry's cheap tricks. Dolly, on the other hand, with the constant attention that came with being in the hospital and her own private garden right in the room, thought she'd been elevated to royalty. Cori smiled at her. Turned upside down in her bed, her tiny feet on the pillow, she talked softly to herself, playing at some secret child's game adults seemed foredoomed to forget. The hale, hearty, pink-cheeked little girl babbling to herself in childhood's language bore scant resemblance to the pale, sickly child who had ridden here in the back of an ambulance. She was again that lively girl who had anticipated a ride upon the magnificent princess horse. It was amazing—and frightening—how quickly she could become one or the other.

But Cori took pride in the fact that she was getting better at handling these startling metamorphoses. She had shed no tears this time, and yet had managed to descend from that state of enhanced clearheadedness, which was for her indicative of extreme anxiety, without awakening to find herself a resident of a padded cell. It was a great relief not to have to hide her face in a corner and try to sniff in silence, but she had forgone the comfort of Reese's arms in remaining dry-eyed. That, too, was probably for the best, however. He had seemed more shaken by Dolly's asthma attack than she would have expected. In fact, there had been a moment when the look upon his face had frightened her every bit as much as Dolly's distress. She reminded herself, again, that Reese had never before witnessed a full-blown asthmatic reaction, and again she wondered if he blamed himself for what had happened.

He denied any such thought, and she hoped that was true, but there had to be some explanation for the deep blue funk into which he had fallen. He seemed to believe her, to be unaware of it, and he had done a good job each of the past three days of acting his old self.

She glanced at her watch. He would be here soon, if the pattern held true, and she would have the pleasure of telling him they were going home in the morning. It could have been today, but the pediatrician was being extremely cautious. She wanted Dolly well enough within the week to be tested for allergies, and Cori wasn't about to argue with her. In fact, if this episode was anyone's fault, it was hers. She should have seen to it that those tests were scheduled weeks ago. She supposed she'd let herself be lulled into believing they wouldn't be necessary, after all. It was not too unreasonable an assumption: Dolly had done so well up to this point.

There came a tap at the door. She twisted in the uncomfortable plastic chair, but the face that appeared belonged to the charge nurse. More forms, Cori supposed correctly. The nurse left them with her to read and sign. This time the topic was post-release care. She read with interest, initialed the appropriate points, and signed the acknowledgment, tearing it off at its perforation. The rest she folded and put into her purse for future reference. It was then, as she zipped the bag, that the door slowly swung open to reveal him standing there. He looked tired, but he smiled.

"How's it goin', ladies?"

She embarrassed herself, she was so glad to see him, and felt the color rushing to her cheeks. "You startled me." The lie was so thin, she didn't even bother to apologize.

He stepped into the room, just far enough to allow the door to clear as it swung shut, and looked around. "Seems Jerry sent a whole florist's shop."

She felt herself smile stiffly. "He tends to go overboard."

He seemed to think on that, which was in itself a strange thing, and slipped his hands into his pockets, pushing back the sides of his suit coat. It was not, she noticed, a particularly flattering costume. The sandy beige color warred with the ice blue of his eyes and his ruddy complexion. She thought again that he looked tired.

"Well," he drawled at last, "at least he doesn't leave any doubt concerning his sentiments."

It sounded to Cori like a very odd remark, for all that it was true and couldn't be argued with. She searched for something safe and sensible to say, but couldn't seem to find an unrelated subject. She did the best she could.

"Um, actually the roses weren't such a good idea," she told him. "The doctor thinks Dolly has allergies that trigger the asthma, and since a lot of people are allergic to flowers…" She lost the train of her thoughts as he turned away and went to the side of the bed.

Dolly had rolled onto her stomach and lifted her face onto the heels of her upturned hands. She smiled up at him, and he nodded in response, though what curled his mouth could not really be described as an expression of gladness or fondness or even humor.

"You seem to be feeling well," he said to the child.

Cori spoke up, miffed at his obvious snub. "She's fine. And at least we now know she isn't allergic to roses."

"That's fortunate," he returned softly, his voice full of an indefinable ache that robbed Cori of even her small anger and left her feeling hopeless.

"I'm going home tomorrow," Dolly said, dropping her hands in order to speak.

"Good for you." He turned to Cori. "I'd be glad to send a car for you."

She felt a deep, bitter disappointment. Was it too much to have hoped he would meet them and escort them home himself? Apparently it was, and she might as well start learning now to accept that fact. "It might be simpler if we just hire a taxi," she managed. He didn't argue.

"Whatever you think best."

Cori's hands tightened on the soft leather purse. Had she only imagined that he cared? She didn't know what to think, but even as she stood there, trying to tell herself that this was not the end of her own personal world, she saw him staring at her hands. At first she thought he was looking at the purse and wondering why she held it so desperately. Then she realized he was staring at her ring, her "engagement" ring.

She wanted to wrench the thing off and throw it out the window. She wanted to shout, "Lie! Lie! Lie!" She wanted to declare that Jerry meant nothing to her, that she did not, could not, love him. She wanted to say, even, that she loved him, Reese. But she didn't dare. His coldness prevented the truth from being shared. Tensely, she turned away and dropped the purse onto the little stand beside the bed.

He stayed awhile longer, looking with feigned interest at the crayon drawings Dolly proudly presented to him. After a few minutes, Dolly asked permission to switch on the television, and Cori granted it. He turned to go, and Corinne accompanied him into the corridor, careful to keep the distance he seemed to need between them.

"What of her mother?" he asked when they were safely beyond hearing. Cori looked at him.

"What of her?"

"Do you know where she is?"

She shook her head. "She'll surface again. She always does. Probably with another husband to add to her collection."

He seemed truly shocked. "Won't you have to send Dolly back to her at some point?"

"No." Her tone left no room for doubt. "Oh, Martina will want to see her again sometime, and I'll let her, but Dolly belongs to me. Everyone knows it. Even Dolly. Perhaps most of all, Dolly."

They came to the end of the corridor, and he stood before the elevator bank, his arms folded across his middle. "Will you have children of your own?"

The question took her completely by surprise. "I don't know," she told him truthfully. "I haven't thought about it."

His mouth fell open, and his eyes narrowed accusingly. "You haven't thought about it! You're engaged to be married and you haven't even thought about whether or not you'll have children?''

His tone stung her. Automatically, she drew herself up in an attitude of defense. What right had he to ask such questions? What right had he to censure her? More important, where had her friend gone? Had Jerry cost her even that? Something of her despair must have shown through her anger, for he suddenly sighed, slumping, and wearily lifted a hand in apology.

"I'm sorry," he said. "It's not my place—" He broke off, grimacing. "I didn't mean to sound, um, judgmental. I-it's just that having a child is such an a-awesome responsibility."

"I know that," she told him, her voice low and terse. "I already *have* a child."

He looked stricken, his face suddenly pale and chalky, his eyes ringed with dark, purplish shadows. He ran a hand over his bristly hair. "I'm glad she's better," he mumbled, and his hand shot out to push the call button for the elevator. At once, a door slid open to his right, and he stepped through it.

Suddenly she was alone, the halves of the door sliding together, and now there were tears on her cheeks. Where was the man whose arms had held her the last time? Where was that great friend about whose love she had dreamed? Gone. Gone. Gone. But whether these were tears of grief for what hadn't been and would not be, or anger at the foolishness that had put this ring on her, she didn't honestly know. She only knew that she was hurt and alone and lonely, except for the little girl down at the end of the hall. Niece or daughter, she was her own little girl, and she was making no apologies about that—to anyone.

She walked slowly back to Dolly's room, drying her cheeks with her fingertips and schooling her expression into a soft smile. She pushed the door open, and the little head, now upon its pillow, turned to greet her. The enormous emerald eyes lit vaguely with what had become a perfunctory greeting, all the more precious precisely because it had become habit. They were a unit now, a family. Whatever happened, they had each other, and always would. Corinne couldn't imagine loving another child any more or less than she loved Dolly, whether a child of her own body or that of a complete stranger. She marveled at herself. Who would have thought that she, Corinne Terral, single career-woman, possessed all this mothering instinct?

"Okay, sweetie," she said, suddenly happy despite the dull, nameless ache in the center of her chest, "what sort of game would you like to play on your last night in the hospital?"

Dolly sat bolt upright in her rumpled bed and cried, "Candyland!"

Cori winced, then laughed. She'd seen the game box on a shelf down in the playroom, right above a red wagon filled with an odd collection of toys. "I'll get it," she said, and turned right around to do just that.

Two hours later, having managed to lose at least half of the six games they'd played, she snuggled into the recliner furnished for that very purpose and stared at a nearly silent television while Dolly slept soundly and peacefully at her side. She felt a sense of contentment which, like Dolly's greeting, had a faithful familiarity to it, and yet the ache was there, vague, amorphous, subtle. She told herself grimly that she could live with it; but then, what other choice did she have?

No matter. It was temporary. There had been no great love affair, after all; just a single kiss, a feeling of connection, a hopefulness.

Suddenly exhausted by it all, she flicked off the television and leaned back, banishing thoughts of Reese into the darkness that engulfed the impersonal room. It was an act of will performed time and again throughout the long night, for sleep eluded her. Yet at last the long night gave way to the rising of the sun, and Corinne got up to ready herself for departure.

She was bathed and dressed long before the breakfast trays came. Dolly woke eager to be off, but somehow Cori got her washed up just in time for the meal. They made the usual jokes about the limp bacon, watery eggs and cardboard toast, consoling themselves with the knowledge that lunch would come from Mrs. Campbell's own capable hands. After the doctor made his morning rounds, Cori called the taxi service and the business office, then left Dolly watching cartoons while she walked down to the nurses' station to try to hurry up the paperwork. A few minutes later, having gathered up their belongings, they walked out the door and down the hall to the elevator.

The taxi was waiting when they stepped out onto the covered sidewalk and into the warm, moist, late-morning air. Dolly wore her bedroom slippers and housecoat, clasping in her arms the one vase of roses Corinne had allowed her to keep, the others to be distributed to remaining patients by the nurses. The dark red blossoms swayed about her little face as she ran with tiny steps to the car door opened by the driver. He was a garrulous sort, laughing and talking every moment, and he came to help Corinne carry their accumulated stuff to the trunk. It was amazing what one collected during a hospital stay with a child: crayons, cards, coloring books, a whistling, plastic top she'd found in the gift shop for Dolly, bedclothes, pillows, magazines, tiny packages of saltines, toiletries in travel sizes, a plastic washbasin and a water pitcher to match, as well as a soap dish and a thermometer holder and a box of cheap tissues. There were other things—personal things brought from the house by Mrs. Campbell and a gift of bath salts Corinne had bought for her because of her thoughtfulness. The woman was a treasure, and Cori felt certain that she would stay full-time with Geneva after she and Dolly had moved on.

Moving on was a topic with which she had long occupied herself during the previous evening, and she had determined to speak to Jerry about it at first opportunity. Perhaps, with Mrs. Campbell's aid, it would not be necessary for them to stay on until Jerry returned. She wondered where they would go, what sort of place she'd be able to afford. So far the only two places she had seen were Jerry's and Reese's, and she knew quite well that neither was representative of what she could look forward to, as both were extreme examples of individual taste, Jerry's all cut up and compartmentalized and decorated with deadly good taste, while Reese's style seemed broad, inclusive and oddly sentimental. One was cool but efficient, while the other seemed warm, detailed, even confusing to the unschooled eye, which would be any but Reese's. What a complex man he was.

She pushed away the thought, bemoaning the circumstance that brought Reese Compton to mind. No matter what she began thinking about, she always ended with thoughts of Reese Compton. She supposed it was indicative of her state of mind—or perhaps her state of heart. She only wished that there was something to be done about it. Obviously, there was not. He plainly regretted his actions the day of the picnic.

The thing between them had evidently played itself out. Well, she'd had no right to expect anything more. It was, in more ways than one, time to begin to think of moving on.

The cabbie talked a stream as he drove them west along the seawall, weaving in and out of the stop-and-go traffic as if he possessed some magical ability to anticipate the actions and position of every other driver in his path. They were home in twenty minutes, and once there, the driver hopped out happily to carry her baggage up those offensive stairs and then, surprisingly, refused not only her payment but also her tip.

"Mr. Compton already took care of it," he told her with a clap of his hands. "He said if you was to object, I should remind you that he'd promised his friend, Mr. Arnold."

Of course. He had promised Mr. Arnold. "I see," she replied as graciously as her wounded feelings would allow. "Well, thank you."

"Best to you and the gal, ma'am," he said, and he left them.

She let herself into the house with her key, using the moment to ease the hurt at being reminded the favor had been for Jerry and not for her. It was foolish to have such feelings, useless, groundless. She and Reese had shared a single kiss, nothing more; and now she could see there was to be no more. The thing to do was to concentrate on Dolly, as she ought to have done from the beginning.

The door opened, and she smiled down at the little face among the roses. Dolly beamed at her and padded inside, calling, "Geneva! Miz Campbell!"

The latter came toddling from the direction of the kitchen, a wooden spoon in her hand, a broad smile upon her plump face. "So we're home and well, are we?"

"And glad to be," Cori told her. "Where's Geneva?"

"On the phone in the den, I believe, with Mr. Jerry."

That sent Corinne's brows up a couple of notches. She found she was actually glad of it. There was, as they said, no time like the present. Leaving Dolly in Mrs. Campbell's capable hands, she hurried across the living room, into the corridor, down the stairs and into the den. Geneva stood with her slightly bowed back to the door, the telephone receiver to her ear, obviously unaware of Corinne's presence.

"I don't know," she was saying. "You'd have to ask Cori or maybe Reese. He might know." She paused and her free hand wandered up to her hair. "Well, because they work together," she said in obvious reply. Then, after a moment, "What's wrong with Cori working for Reese? You work for Reese." She paused for a moment, and Cori recognized consternation in the way she twisted about while he spoke to her. "I don't understand any of this," she said. "Cori wouldn't really do anything to hurt you. Would she?"

Cori could just imagine what he was telling her. How he'd asked his fiancée not to work for Reese, how worried he was because she didn't understand Reese, how she might say the wrong thing and how it could be taken the wrong way. Of course, he wouldn't remind his mother that it was his own lies that he feared would be exposed. He wouldn't admit how he'd tried to manipulate everyone.

Geneva was twisting the cord of the phone where it connected to the receiver, obviously troubled. "Well, I don't know," she said. "I'll try. I just don't know." He must have said something soothing then because her tone abruptly changed. "Yes, of course, my dear. Of course. Of course. I'm sure that once you're home again, all will be well. I'm certain of it."

What followed was nothing more than the banal pleasantries one uses to end a conversation. Cori waited until she was quite done and the receiver was once again fitted into its receptacle, her very just anger at Jerry held carefully in check. "Geneva."

The older woman turned, her movements short and laborious. "Cori," she said, her smile genuine.

Corinne sighed. "You were talking to Jerry just now, weren't you?" she asked evenly.

At that reminder, Geneva's pleasant expression froze. "He's very concerned about you," she said, her wobbling chin held aloft.

"More concerned about what I might tell," Corinne corrected. "Geneva, you mustn't let him manipulate you."

"Manipulate me?" She was genuinely shocked. "He's my son, he wouldn't . . ." She couldn't seem to remember what he wouldn't do. Instead, she was remembering what Corinne might do. "If you really love him—"

"I don't love him!" Corinne cried, exasperated with the whole situation. "And he knows it! This whole engagement is a farce! It's his lie, and I've protected him from it. And if he wasn't so intent on using you, he'd remind you of that fact!"

Geneva glared at her, then suddenly her face crumpled. "I'm so confused," she mewled. "Everyone's mad at me."

Cori at once regretted her outburst. Groaning, she hurried forward and slipped her arm about the older woman's bent shoulders. "No one's mad at you," she said. "It's just that it's not your problem, you know? Leave it to Jerry and me. Please?"

The older woman sniffed and nodded. "That's just what I'll do," she said. "I'll stay out of it. I—I'll stay in my room."

"You don't have to do that," Cori began, but Geneva was hurrying away, having found her solution.

Cori let her go, trusting that she would soon forget the whole episode and silently rebuking herself for having spoken. Jerry was the culprit, not Geneva, but she'd be damned if she was going to put up with it indefinitely. Angrily, she jerked the diamond from her finger and closed it in her fist. She would not wear it again, and she would answer all inquiries about its absence honestly. She would do or say nothing purposely to hurt Jerry, but she would not go on pretending any longer. The engagement was done, finished, and if he cared to argue the point, she would simply let out the whole truth and let him sink or swim by his own weight.

And if Jerry couldn't handle the knowledge that she was working for Compton, that was his problem. She felt lighter by pounds rather than mere karats, and she took the ring upstairs where she left it by his bed on the nightstand, free at last. *Now,* she mused wryly, *when it can make no difference.*

"Jerry Arnold on line one," Evelyn's voice announced.

Reese scowled and leaned back in his chair, glaring at the offending instrument for a full ten seconds, then pulled himself together and reached for the receiver. After placing it to his ear, he punched the blinking button.

"Reese Compton here."

"Top Gun!"

Jerry's voice was full of feigned enthusiasm. Reese forced himself to relax.

"Hello, Jerry. How's it going?"

"Great! We've started work on the final plans."

Reese blanched. That meant they were well ahead of schedule. Normally, this would be good news, even fantastic news, but Reese couldn't help thinking that once

Jerry's duties were fulfilled he would be returning home to marry Corinne Terral. *Well, it's what you want, isn't it?* he reminded himself. *Better him than you.*

He tried to listen as Jerry filled him in on the particulars of the project, but his thoughts were elsewhere. How could this jerk so cavalierly accept responsibility for a child not even his? Or did he? Chances were he hadn't even given a second thought to Dolly. Perhaps he even expected that her mother would return for her at some point, thus leaving him with Cori all to himself. Reese ground his teeth in consternation, then abruptly called a halt to his thoughts. It was none of his business. Corinne belonged to Jerry. And Dolly belonged to Corinne. Period.

He interrupted Jerry in midsentence, eager to be done with the conversation and turn his thoughts elsewhere. "Sounds like you've got everything under control, Jer, as usual. Do you need anything from this end?"

"Well, now that you mention it . . ."

Reese all but groaned aloud, realizing too late that he'd left himself wide open. Jerry continued.

"I'm afraid I owe you an apology. It seems we've taken advantage of your generous spirit already."

Some of the dread he was feeling dissipated, and he allowed himself a light tone. "I can't imagine how."

"It's Cori," Jerry said, and Reese immediately tensed again. "I didn't realize that she'd come to you for work. I only just learned of it. Believe me, Reese, I never intended for that to happen. In fact, I pointedly told her *not* to do it."

Was that all? Reese let out a silent sigh, shaking his head at Jerry's overblown concern. "She did mention that to me . . ." he began, but Jerry was obviously trying to make a point, and he wasn't going to be distracted.

"You know how women are. They sometimes approach the business community like it was a big bridge club."

Reese frowned at the sexist remark but said nothing, allowing Jerry to go on.

"I'd take this up with Cori herself, but that little niece of hers has been in the hospital recently. Well, you probably know all about that. The point is, this is a bad time for a serious conversation with Cori, so I thought perhaps you and I could rectify the situation ourselves, sort of man-to-man, you know? I promise I'll speak to Cori about this and see that it doesn't happen again. Meanwhile I'd appreciate it if we could just keep this between us."

Reese was steaming. He wanted to tell the creep that "that little niece of hers" was named Dolly and that she was a real person. He wanted to yell at the idiot that Dolly, dear, sweet child that she was, had very nearly died! And further, he could've told the bozo that Cori was every bit as capable an engineer as *he* was, and a damned sight more sensitive and caring, not to mention professional, principled, and . . . He swallowed his outrage and made himself think logically.

"What, exactly, is it that you want kept just between us, Jerry?" The hard edge of his voice seemed to have communicated itself, for Jerry's next words were cautious, measured.

"What I thought, that is, what seems best is for you— er, rather the company—simply to find no more projects for her."

"That's what you think is best?" Reese's tone was terse, his words clipped. "You want me to cut Cori out and keep mum that you instigated the whole thing?"

Jerry was obviously ruffled. "I, er, um, just meant that you should, ah, do whatever was most convenient—for you, I mean."

"And you assume the most convenient thing for me to do is to snub Cori until she gets the idea that her help isn't wanted around here, right?"

There came an audible gulp over the line. It gave Reese no small measure of satisfaction.

"Hey, Top," Jerry said, speaking quickly, "I didn't mean to imply that you should do anything you consider improper. I just wanted you to know that you don't have to let Cori go on imposing on you for *my* sake. If you like, I'll speak to her about it. I'm just asking you to understand that now is not a good time for it."

Reese had to hand it to him; Jerry Arnold knew how to land on his feet. Pity. At the moment Reese wanted nothing more than a good excuse to fire the cad. But nothing that had been said or done justified such an action. Whatever his faults, Jerry was a top-notch engineer and an excellent manager, and the truth was that Reese's own feelings were based on nothing more than jealousy and guilt—and plenty of it. Suddenly he wondered if the most honorable thing at this point wouldn't be to just admit openly that he was in love with Corinne.

And then what? Beg Jerry's forgiveness? Not for hell or high water. Besides, confession wouldn't solve anything for him. He just wasn't ready for the kind of risk loving meant, especially not with a child involved. He wiped a hand over his face. Jerry Arnold had nothing on him when it came to being a creep.

"You're worrying about nothing," he told Jerry, trying to smooth the rough edges from his tone. "Corinne's work has been excellent. She's been no imposition at all. At any rate, I wouldn't do as you suggest. It just isn't good business etiquette. Besides which, Cori deserves better. Now, if that's all . . ."

"Sure. Whatever you say. I just wanted you to understand that I tried to do what I felt was right. I'm, uh, glad the two of you have hit it off so well."

Now what was *that?* Suspicion? Reese sat staring at his desktop, trying to decide just what this call was really about. Finally, he came to the conclusion that it didn't matter. Even if Jerry did suspect that he was attracted to Cori, nothing would come of it because the attraction would come to nothing. He couldn't let it. He didn't dare.

He said something, anything, to get Jerry off the phone and hung up. He reached for a file, any file, that would occupy his thoughts and attention. His hand fell on a manila folder in his In box. He brought it before him and opened it. The cover sheet read, "Recommendation for Promotion. Re: The London Chair."

He knew what he was going to see before he even turned the page, but he turned it anyway, some perverse sense of justice goading him. He skipped over the opening addresses and greetings and went right to the heart of the letter.

It said everything he'd expected it to: Jerry Arnold was the man for the job. Quickly, he skimmed three other memos. All had reached the same conclusion, and with work proceeding ahead of schedule on the Brazilian project, he had to agree. Jerry, being as ambitious as he was competent, would probably jump at this opportunity. And Cori and Dolly might well be so far out of sight as to be *almost* out of mind. Almost.

He knew he was going to have to bring Jerry in on this now. It might be for the best, anyway. With an ocean between them, maybe he could stop thinking about Cori as if he had some right to. Maybe he could get that picture of

Dolly, white-faced and gasping for air, out of his head. God, if only he weren't such a rotten coward! What grown man in his right mind would fear a little girl and her asthma? One who'd lost a child already, said a voice inside his head. It chilled him right down to the bone.

He'd get the letter off today, informing Jerry that he had been suggested for the London chair and inviting a reply. And, he decided grimly, he'd send out a cautious word to P & S: Miss Terral's service was to be phased out. She was about to become a married woman, after all, and her husband would likely find himself transferred to a distant post. He could keep it from looking too suspicious or unfair. Now if he could just make himself feel better about it ... If he could just forget her, *them* ... He had to. Somehow, he just had to. He already had all the haunting memories he could stand.

Chapter Nine

"London!" Jerry had said. "Think of it! Wouldn't you like to live there? Wouldn't it be a broadening experience for your little Dolly?"

Of course, she'd have to marry him in order to make that happen, but to Jerry that was a mere trifle when compared with the benefits of living in Europe. Why, weren't they as good as engaged anyway?

He'd had a fit when she'd told him she was no longer wearing his ring. How could she do this to him? he had wanted to know. Didn't she realize she could knock him out of this promotion if word got to Reese that they were no longer engaged?

"Balderdash!" she had said. She said it again now, yanking the laces of her running shoes tight. "Balderdash."

With that she rose and began to warm up. Knees flexed, arms extended, she slowly bent forward, flattening her back and stretching her spine. She counted aloud, but her mind was still with Jerry and his incredible conceit. Did he really think that he could convince her to marry him? She shook her head, losing track of the count, and started over again.

"One, two, three, four..."

Apparently Jerry labored under the delusion that once a woman became enamored of him, she never again regained her sense. He'd even had the gall to appeal to her "more womanly instincts."

"I need you," he'd said. "Mother needs you. Think of it, Cori. Could you send us to London alone, knowing how deeply we've come to depend upon you? It's your nature to nurture. Look at Dolly! You've upended your life to play the mother figure for her, but wouldn't it be best for her to be part of a real family? And married to me, you'd never need to work again. You'd be free to follow your more womanly instincts."

She'd followed that sexist, patronizing, ill-conceived speech by slamming down the phone, and she'd slammed it down twice more since then. The lunatic still didn't understand what he'd said wrong. Never need to work again! As if mothering were not work enough! As if her career were somehow more disposable than his! As if she couldn't follow her "more womanly instincts" and hold her place in the business world, too! Well, Jerry Arnold could go soak his head, and she didn't care one whit if he did it in Brazil or London or Antarctica. Not that she didn't wish him well.

She flopped down and stretched one long leg out before her, reaching for her toes. She really didn't want to see Jerry in trouble. He worked hard, and however irritating she found his courtship methods, he had provided her a haven in a moment of crisis. But she wasn't about to allow herself to be manipulated by him one moment longer.

She had no intention of exposing the engagement for the fraud that it was, but she wasn't going to perpetuate the fraud any longer, either. The so-called engagement was off, but she'd protect him from the truth if she could. She wanted him to get this promotion, and not only for his sake. She wanted to stay on the island, now that her business was finally taking off. Despite everything, she and Dolly had been happy here. They were going to start apartment hunting soon. She wanted to be settled in firmly before school started.

She got up and stretched her arms high above her head, filling her lungs with cool, Sunday-morning air. What was it about Sunday mornings that made them seem so clean and peaceful? She'd first started these morning runs on a Sunday, and the result had been a definite lifting of the dark mood that had assailed her when she'd realized that her personal connection with Compton Engineering had been severed. It didn't take a genius to figure out that she was being dumped.

One day she couldn't do enough for them, the next they had nothing for her. She had been despondent and not only because she'd counted on the work. Reese had obviously canceled their friendship, too—or whatever it was that had drawn them together. But that had been nearly three weeks ago. This was today, and today she had the security of a major contract with another firm, as well as several smaller ones—enough to guarantee her business for the next year or better. By then, there would be more. Of that, she was confident.

But that was tomorrow. This was today, and today she was going to run the beach while the gulf breezes still cooled it. Later, the sun would warm it to near baking temperature, and people would fling themselves down prone to soak up the hot rays, covering the sand with their oily bodies.

Her stretching done, she bent to straighten the cuff of her socks, then tugged at the high-cut leg of her maillot. She had quickly learned the benefits of running on the beach in a swimsuit. They were positively addicting. Happily, she set out, striking a smooth, easy stride that carried her across the yard, out into the street, and along the side of the narrow dirt road. Within minutes she was crossing the Seawall Boulevard and striking down the sandy trail to the beach. The running was more arduous in the sand, but more beneficial, too. The ground soaked up a greater portion of the impact, and the strides required more energy, which burned more calories and had a more toning effect on the muscles.

Once gaining the open beach, she turned west, away from the city itself and its commercial beachfronts. Her chances of running into anyone else at this time of the morning were slim, but they were greater the farther east one went, so she habitually chose the western route.

She hadn't covered a half-dozen yards when she saw him, a tiny, solitary figure in pale blue huddled against the sharp morning breeze. At first, he was nothing more than a blue speck, not even a he, really; just a someone sitting on the sand. As she drew nearer, she thought that it was a child, but no, the proportion was all wrong. This was a bigger person, a person in a blue T-shirt. Make that a windbreaker. This was an adult person in a pale blue windbreaker. Soon thereafter she settled upon the sex: definitely male. No woman would wear her hair *that* short.

She ran on, her stride choppier in the deep sand than on the hard-packed road, while *he* stared out to sea, completely unaware, apparently, that he was no longer alone. She rather enjoyed the harmless voyeurism, the secret feel of seeing but remaining unseen, until he turned his face in her direction and the shock of instant recognition rocked her. Reese. Even at this distance she knew him. And he knew her. She saw his quick, involuntary turn away. She steeled herself and moved her gaze to the edge of the water. She didn't have to acknowledge him. She didn't have to stop. He'd made his preference plain with three weeks of absence, with a lack of work, with his silence. Her heart was working twice as hard as seemed necessary, but she was determined to manage this. They both lived on the island, after all. They were bound to run into one another from time to time. Besides, they weren't enemies. They just weren't friends any longer. Nodding acquaintances, she decided. They were nodding acquaintances. That being the case, she would nod unceremoniously as she passed by him. Except that she couldn't do it.

She just couldn't make herself look in his direction, let alone nod as if they'd met one day at the grocery and then gone their separate ways. But neither could she manage to pass him there as if he were a stranger, as if he'd never touched her life, let alone her heart. Before she even got to him, she'd somehow lost her stride. Resigned, even resentful, she walked the last few steps, her gaze trained on her own feet. She stood before him, each of them looking anywhere but at the other, while the ocean quietly washed the shore and withdrew again.

Strangely, the atmosphere began to ease, and after a few moments she felt his gaze upon her. The breeze gusted, chilling her now that she no longer exerted herself, and his hand reached up for hers unerringly. A gentle warmth spread through her, heating her whole body in a slow, single stroke. Sighing, she looked down at him, affection rising in her even as she acknowledged her folly in caring for this proud, private, mysterious man. The shadow of a smile crossed his lips. He gave her hand a tug, and she turned slightly, sinking onto the sand at his side, her knees drawn up before her, ankles crossed. She laid her head upon his shoulder, and he tilted his own until his cheek met the crown of her head. They sat just so for some time, hands clasped, staring in concert out to sea. Finally, he spoke.

"How have you been?"

She straightened and fortified herself with a deep breath. "Okay."

"Dolly?"

She noticed his voice was thick and dull, so much so that she took a moment to study his face before replying. He didn't look at her, but instead drew a curving mark in the sand with the forefinger of his free hand.

"Dolly's well," she said, finding no reason or name for this emotion he displayed. He nodded, and she went on. "She had the allergy tests last week. They're not strictly conclusive yet, but we know she's allergic to dust and gerbils and a variety of pollens. We'll see what else comes up, develop an antitoxin and start her on shots, and in a couple of weeks we're both going to a class on managing asthma in preadolescents. I guess you could say we're progressing. At any rate, to look at her today, you wouldn't know she'd ever had a health problem."

He drew another shape in the sand, then squinted out to sea. "That would be the scariest part for me," he said slowly. "Never knowing from one moment to the next." He went back to his sand drawing, concentrating with such intensity that his next question took her completely by surprise. "Have you thought about what you'll do if something happens to her?"

She didn't know what he meant at first, couldn't fathom the catch in his voice or the sudden tightness of his hand on hers. And then she knew he was asking about death. The idea stunned. She couldn't even imagine what she would do, but she knew that Dolly had filled her world with love; and nothing, not even death, could take that away.

"I suppose," she answered him slowly, "I'd do what everyone else does when they lose someone they love."

He shook his head, and the eyes he turned on her were narrow and red with pain and a kind of knowledge she hadn't suspected he possessed. "It was a foolish question," he said. "You can't know until it happens. You think you can, but you can't, not really."

He lapsed into silence again, suffering with some inexplicable grief. She didn't know what to say, so she simply sat there and gripped his hand in hers, waiting for the moment to pass. Gradually, he seemed to relax.

"How's Geneva?" he asked, trying for a light tone.

"The same, I suppose. Maybe a little better. I'm not sure." She didn't say that she couldn't be sure because Geneva hardly spoke to her anymore. Geneva didn't mean to be difficult; she just didn't know how she was supposed to act anymore. The one thing she seemed to understand was that Cori would not marry her son. Cori understood her ambivalence and why they'd settled into an amiable if slightly strained silence. Reese didn't seem to want to pursue Geneva's well-being any more than she did, so they left it there and moved on.

They rose, and he steered her westward, placing himself between her and the wind whispering over the sea to land. They walked in tandem, no longer clasping hands, the uneasiness returning. She wanted to speak, but decided it would be best to wait him out. They'd gone a quarter of a mile before he said anything.

"Are you working?" he asked, the words so laden with guilt that they tore at her heart.

"Yes. I'm very busy, as a matter of fact. I registered with an agency, and they've found me several contracts, including one really big design job I'm very excited about."

That seemed to help a bit. He stopped and ran his hands over his hair, not yet daring to look at her again. "I'm sorry. I'm so very sorry."

"About what?" she returned quietly. "About not having work for me? That's just the way it goes sometimes. I understand."

"Do you?" he asked skeptically. "Do you really?"

She turned away, feeling his eyes upon her, unable to meet them. "No," she admitted in a small, trembling voice, and suddenly tears welled in her eyes. He put his arms around her from the back and stepped up close, bringing the wall of his chest against her shoulder blades.

"Do you understand now?" he whispered, nuzzling the dark hair at her temple.

Her eyelids dropped in a silent prayer of hope, tears at bay, breath bated. *He wants me,* she tried to assure herself, but she had to know. She had to be sure. Swallowing hard, she shook her head.

He felt hot all along her length, but he'd been in the cold water this morning. His light brown swim trunks were still damp, and his upper body was bare beneath the thin fabric of the windbreaker. When had he gone in? An hour ago? Just before daylight? She wanted to know, to *feel* everything that had happened to him.

He turned her roughly then, his hands upon her arms, and his mouth crashed down against hers, demanding, violent, even bitter. She let him have his way, sure of herself for the first time, confident of him, understanding everything, trusting. He did not disappoint her. Gradually his mouth softened, and the steel bands of his hands loosened and moved to cup her face. She lifted her arms about him then and felt his embrace close around her, his hands gently kneading the flesh over which they moved. She leaned against him, her head lighting upon his shoulder, face turned up to his, mouth opening to accept the claim of his tongue. She fitted herself to him, plane to plane, mound to valley. They were like two pieces of a puzzle, the picture whole only when they were fitted together, their bodies complementing one another.

She had never been so sure of anything. She loved this man, and he loved her. He must. Nothing short of love would drive him to abandon that ironclad, militaristic code of honor by which he lived. Mere lust could never produce in him the determination to break the smallest promise; yet he had promised her work and taken it away. He had promised to call and had not. He had promised Jerry that he would keep a close eye on her, but it had been more than three weeks since she'd seen him. And now here he stood, believing that she was Jerry's fiancée, his arms holding her tight, his mouth mated to hers and manipulating with a hunger so raw and deep and overpowering that even as she celebrated her certainty, she clung to him in fear. He loved her, but he was not hers, and yet more hers than she was Jerry's.

Slowly, she began to pull away from him, but Reese clasped her to him with a desperation bordering on anger, so that in the end it was he who wrenched away, his disgust—for whom, she didn't know—so thick as to be palpable. Before she could speak or even comprehend what was happening, he was striding away, arms straight at his sides, back as rigid as a girder.

"Reese!"

He made no response at all, no flinch, no pause, no sound. She watched, mouth agape, but somehow she knew his pain was greater, deeper. She put a hand to her head, so confused about what she should do that she could do nothing. He continued walking, receding until he was nothing more than that tiny speck she'd first seen on the beach. Gasping air, she wiped her eyes and turned away, forcing herself to pick up first one foot and then another, running for all she was worth, toward what she didn't know, except that it had to be a solution because she couldn't lose him now. She needed him, and more than that, she wanted him. She couldn't lose him now. She couldn't.

Over and over again, she told herself how it was. She loved him—good, kind, tender man that he was. He loved her, but he thought her out of reach, owing to a foolish lie and his own hard pride, virtue and sense of honor. He imagined himself a scoundrel for falling in love with another man's woman, perhaps even a weakling, and such circumstance could turn love to hate. She couldn't let that happen, and even as she ran, turning finally toward the bayou road, she racked her brain for how best to accomplish her goal. He must be made to listen. Somehow she had to make him understand that he had betrayed nothing and no one. She had never been Jerry's in the first place, and he must understand that. It was only as the house came into view, its sharp, haughty angles reminding her of Jerry, that she knew who would have to tell him.

She turned down the drive and trotted the last yards, coming to a halt before the despised stairs. Breathless, exhausted, she took a moment to recoup her strength. Then doggedly, grimly, she mounted the steps and climbed, let herself in the front door and moved swiftly, silently through the entry. She turned left into the dining room, then pushed through swinging doors to enter the pantry and out again on the other side to the kitchen.

Mrs. Campbell was there, humming to herself as she slid deep, flaky biscuits from a baking sheet to a tray for their breakfast. She was dressed for church but had stopped off to see to it that they ate properly before going on to services. She seemed to think them incapable of fending for themselves, and they had become awfully spoiled by her constant attention. Cori wondered if the Arnolds would take her with them to London, or if she would even be willing to go. She hoped for Geneva's sake that Mrs. Campbell would go with them. The woman was a genuine treasure.

Cori spared her a smile as she reached for the phone, lifting it from its receptacle bolted to the wall. Quickly, she punched in the many numbers and settled down on a stool to wait. After a very long time, a hollow, clacking sound came over the wire. An arrangement of clicks, whirs and screeches followed, and finally a muted buzz broken at intervals by a tinny silence. She was about to hang up, disappointment beginning to triumph over determination, when the connection was made and a lazy feminine voice greeted her.

"Sí? Señor Ar-rnald's casa."

Cori's brows went up in surprise, but she didn't bother to speculate about who this woman might be. There were many legitimate possibilities, but she didn't really care what the explanation might be, whether she was housekeeper or lover, as long as she spoke English.

"Mr. Arnold, please."

"¿Que?"

Well, so much for that. She took a deep breath, trying to remember every Spanish phrase she'd ever heard. Not much came to mind. "Mis-ter Ar-nold," she persisted. "I wish to speak to Mis—ah, Señor Ar-nold."

After several moments the woman came back on the line, sounding as if she were reading phonetically. "Uh, Señor Ar-rnald no can spek. Señor Ar-rnald no . . . no he-yar."

Cori sighed, then raised her voice, speaking slowly and distinctly. "I want to leave a message. A message? I want to leave a message for Señor Arnold."

"*Sí.*"

"*Sí,*" Cori echoed under her breath. "I hope." She cleared her throat. "Tell Señor Arnold to call, uh, telephone, Cori. Did you get that? Señor Arnold is to telephone Cori."

"*Sí,*" the feminine voice came back. "*Teléfono Cor-ri.*"

"Right. Señor Arnold telephone-o Cori."

"*Sí, sí. Teléfono Cor-ri.*"

"Great. Thank you, uh, *gracias.* Goodbye."

"*Sí, teléfono Cor-ri.*"

Cori hung up, considering herself lucky to have communicated the message at all and trusting that the other party wouldn't be offended even if she hadn't understood "goodbye." Now all she had to do was settle in and wait for Jerry to call, so naturally she felt like pacing the floor. Mrs. Campbell noticed immediately and set a saucer bearing a buttered biscuit in front of her.

"I shouldn't eat this," Cori said, but the aroma was heavenly. She picked it up and sank her teeth into it. Melted butter dropped onto her fingers and chin. She savored every sinful bite, then took her slick fingers off for a shower. Half an hour later, wrapped in a fluffy pink terry-cloth robe, her wet hair hanging down her back, she carried the Sunday papers into her room, pulled the armchair close to the window, propped her bare feet on the sill and began to read. But her thoughts and eyes kept straying to the slim blue telephone on her bedside table.

Geneva and Dolly got up, the latter coming in to nuzzle in her lap a moment before skipping off to have her breakfast, and then returning a bit later to ask if she could accompany Mrs. Campbell to church. Cori offered to help her dress, but it seemed that Mrs. Campbell, having anticipated Cori's answer, was already running Dolly's bath and laying out her clothes. Deprived of any other distraction, Cori went back to the newspapers. She'd worked all the way through the stack to the classifieds when a ringing sound propelled her out of her seat.

She went automatically to the phone, but an instant later realized what she'd heard was the doorbell. Rolling her eyes, she wrapped the robe tighter about her and hurried out into the hall. The bell rang again. Irritably, she punched the button on the intercom as she went by, calling, "I'm coming. I'm coming."

She padded through the living room, wrenching her robe belt tighter. It occurred to her only as she stepped up into the entry that she didn't have to answer. In fact, she probably ought not to, considering how she was dressed; but if she didn't, then Geneva would. Besides, she didn't have anything better to do.

"Why," she muttered at the door, "weren't you the damned phone?" She yanked it open and stepped back, stunned to find Reese there. He wore navy blue slacks, a pale yellow polo shirt—and a troubled expression. She felt his eyes flick over her and felt suddenly bare; her hands went automatically to her collar. His gaze snapped up, and his face paled. He straightened his shoulders.

"We need to talk," he announced brusquely, and marched past her. She clutched her robe tightly, unbidden memories of what had happened earlier at the beach rushing over her. She closed the door, her heart beating hard and fast, and followed him into the living room. He stood in the middle of the floor, a hand lifted to his temple. She waited, and after a moment he turned to face her, pivoting rigidly on one heel. "I owe you an apology."

She shook her head. "Not necessary."

"I think it is."

"All right, have it your way." She folded her arms. "Just tell me what you owe me an apology for."

He looked like a schoolboy who'd been assigned a particularly difficult piece of recitation. He took a deep breath and said, "I can't see you anymore."

No! she wanted to scream. But instead she said calmly, as if offering him a glass of soda, "I don't love Jerry."

Everything seemed to come to an abrupt halt. He stared at her, eyes wide and his hands at his sides. Then suddenly everything seemed to start up again. He blinked, pushed his hands into the pockets of his pants and sighed.

"I know. I think maybe I've known it, or at least sensed it, from the very beginning. Believe me, it doesn't make this any easier."

She trembled inside the terry robe. He wouldn't look at her. She walked across the floor and sat down on the sofa, feeling a bit light-headed. Nothing seemed to make much sense at the moment, but she feared that everything soon would. "Go on," she urged weakly, and he began to pace.

"You may know that I was married once," he said, and she nodded.

She'd heard somewhere that his wife had died, and her impression was that it had happened a long time ago. "I assumed you didn't want to talk about it," she said softly.

He stopped and looked at her, raw pain sculpting his features into sharp planes and angles.

"I think she may have killed herself. There was no good explanation for the accident, and she'd never fully recovered from..." He stopped and swallowed.

Cori hoped he wouldn't go on, and yet she knew she had to hear this, whatever it cost either of them.

He clasped his hands together behind his back. "We had a son," he said quietly. "He died a year before his mother."

The awful reality of what he'd said blinded her for a moment. She stared up at him, not seeing him at all and certainly not hearing him. She thought of Dolly in the back of that ambulance, all limp and pale and silent, and then she thought of losing her, of having to say goodbye, of going on without her.... Her heart felt as if it were twisting to pieces, and she knew this was nothing compared with the reality of actually losing one's child. Dear God, how did people survive it? How had Reese survived it? Reese. She got up and went immediately to put her arms about him.

For a moment he clung to her, saying, "...prone to bronchial infections and colds. You know the sort of thing. But we didn't expect him to die. Even when they told us he had pneumonia, we just didn't expect... I mean, we knew he was sick, and we knew he'd be uncomfortable and frightened, and of course we wanted to spare him as much as we could, to comfort him, reassure him. But almost from the beginning, almost from the moment he went into the hospital, he just lay there, choking and coughing and trying to breathe."

Trying to breathe. She knew what that was like, watching a child gasp and struggle for breath. She knew exactly what that was like. She'd seen that very thing happen with Dolly. *He* had seen that very thing happen with Dolly. Suddenly it all fell into place: the things he'd said in the ambulance, that uncharacteristic look of panic, his sudden coolness toward them afterward, the odd statements, the prolonged absence. She wanted to hold him and tell him it was all right—that *they* were all right, but he was already putting her from him, his hands gently removing hers.

"If I had known..." he was saying. "She's a wonderful child—so like you, so caring—and I commend you for what you're doing, but I haven't the courage to do it myself, Cori. I just can't get involved. I can't. If I cared less—for her, I mean—maybe then. But I just don't know, and I don't suppose it really matters, anyway."

He seemed to slump, to sigh, as if a great weight had been lifted from him, while she trembled, wild-eyed, beneath the burden of a truth she had not expected. She had known that he was scarred by previous experience, that the personal attention he had at times showered on her was the exception rather than the norm for him. She had sensed his aloofness, his reserve, his protective silence; but rarely had she experienced them. It had seemed that she alone had come near the real man—until now.

What she hadn't suspected, and what even he hadn't realized, was how close to him Dolly had come. Cori imagined the moment when he must have thought he'd lost her, the moment when she'd most reminded him of the son who was no more. She shuddered.

Then, folding her hands to stop their tremor, she faced him dispassionately. "I don't know what to say to you. We've never spoken of love, but it has seemed to me that something quite wonderful binds us together—something I've not felt with any other man. I had hoped that you felt it, too, and that it was enough to see us through any adversity. Then it seemed that you could put me—*us*—aside with little effort, and I called myself a romantic fool. But this morning I believed again. And now you come to say you can't get involved." She shook her head, chin high. "What do you want me to believe? That you don't love me? That you *can't* love Dolly? Or that our love means less to you than a painful memory? And if that's true, any of it, where were your high and mighty ideals when you let yourself play the lover to another man's fiancée?"

If she'd struck him, he wouldn't have been half so wounded. The pain made him brutal.

"I let myself fall in love with you because deep down I couldn't believe you really belonged with him, but I didn't know about *her* then. I didn't know she was part of it! If I'd known, I would never have let this happen!"

"Are you so sure you could have stopped it?" she demanded, but he was hurting too badly to rationalize. He just wanted it over with. She could see that, and it frightened her.

"What does it matter?" he murmured indifferently.

"Because," she told him fiercely, "if you could have stopped yourself, if you can stop yourself from loving me now, then what you feel for me is nothing like what I feel for you!"

He lifted his eyes to hers. They seemed paler than ever, drained of all but the barest hint of color. He swallowed with some difficulty, and his mouth twisted in a wry smile. It was then that she realized how tenuous his composure was, how near he was to breaking himself into a million sharp pieces.

"I thank you for that," he said carefully, "despite what it does to me to know that we might have..." He stopped and covered his face with both hands, then abruptly dropped them again. "Don't you see, Cori? For me, love is a choice between miseries. I'm just trying to pick one I can survive!"

"You're assuming that she's going to die!" she argued.

"I have to!" he cried. "I can't take a chance that she won't!"

She stared at him, utterly defeated. Didn't he see that love always carried the possibility of tragedy with it? One could not love without being vulnerable to loss. It *required* risk by its very nature! But he knew that—and rejected it.

"You're not afraid of losing Dolly," she told him flatly. "You're afraid of loving anyone! And that pretty much puts the joke on me, doesn't it? I thought you were so strong, so wise, so deep! But now I wonder what excuse would you find if Dolly were still with her mother? Would you ever have let yourself come close to me if you hadn't believed I was safely promised to another man?" She had hit her mark, for what it was worth. He stood silent, stripped bare by his own self-disgust. She winced, regretting her handiwork. "Perhaps," she whispered, "the joke's on both of us."

He stayed there, saying nothing, looking dazed, and tears sprang to her eyes. She turned away.

"Cori," he began in a ragged voice, but mercifully the phone rang.

She straightened, grasping at straws, fighting to preserve her dignity. "I'll have to get that," she managed to say. "You'd better go. We've said too much already." The jangle came again, but she made no move to answer it. He stirred, but a third ring set her teeth on edge. "Please!" she gasped, and in one prolonged moment he was gone, the door closing with a thud behind him.

She sank onto the couch, her head in her hands. Silence. Lonely, lonely silence. The phone had even stopped ringing, but she'd already forgotten it, anyway. Besides, what did it matter now? She caught her breath and held it, as if by holding the air in her lungs she could hold herself together. But then the first sob broke free, and for a long while she was lost.

Chapter Ten

Cori swung a bare foot over the arm of the chair and sighed, her head rolling to one side. She looked at the computer sitting idle in its efficient nook, and felt a sharp stab of guilt; but still, it wasn't enough to make her get up and do what she ought to. She hadn't pressed a key all day. In fact, she hadn't done *anything* all day, though she constantly told herself she wouldn't allow this depression to go on.

Dolly came into the den, busy with two Barbie dolls, one of which had had a most unflattering haircut at some earlier date. She was wearing raggedy cutoffs and a T-shirt that had seen better days. Her dark hair was slipping free of the loose ponytail into which Cori had swept it that morning. All in all, she looked a lot like Cori herself, right down to the paleness of her face and the hollowness about her startling eyes. Cori knew her own sadness had communicated itself to this sensitive child, and her guilt deepened.

"Come here, darling," she said, trying on a warm smile. Dolly snuggled into the corner of the armchair, her head on Cori's breast. Cori combed the child's bangs with her fingers. "Want to play a game?" Silent, Dolly shook her head, and Cori's spirits promptly plummeted, but she forced herself to rally. "Well then, my angel girl, what would you like to do?" Dolly's little shoulders went up and down in a shrug.

"Is Geneva mad at us?" Dolly asked suddenly.

The question took Cori off guard. She blinked, mind racing. How astute this child was. Cori held her close.

"No, darling. She's not angry. She's much too kind for that. I think she's just confused about something I did, and she's avoiding me because she doesn't know what to say."

"What did you do?"

"Well… It's more what I won't do. You see, Jerry thinks he would like to marry me, and while he's very kind and generous, I just don't think I'd like to marry him, and so, of course, I had to tell him so. It's made things awkward for everyone, but it's nothing for you to worry about."

"Why don't you want to marry him?" the little inquisitor quizzed, and Cori swallowed hard.

"Well, because I don't love him the way a woman ought to love a man she wants to marry. Marriage is supposed to be forever, you know, so you have to be very sure before you do it."

Dolly cocked her head to one side. "My mommy gets married all the time!" she said.

Cori's mouth fell open. "Yes. I suppose she does, but—"

Dolly began to giggle, demonstrating an understanding and tolerance far beyond her years. "Daddy Pope said

Mommy would marry the grocery boy if he was making good tips.''

"That man wasn't your daddy," Cori clarified evenly. "And he's as confused as your mother. Besides, I'm me, not anyone else, and I intend to do it right the first time or not at all."

"Good," Dolly said. "I wouldn't want lots and lots of uncles, too."

She looked up at Cori with such trust that Cori's heart did a flip-flop. She hugged the girl, tears coming to her eyes. What Dolly couldn't know was how slim her chances had become of *ever* having an uncle. Reese Compton, Cori admitted with a sigh, was a hard act to follow. She bit her lip, holding thoughts of him at bay.

"Are you going to cry again?" Dolly asked from the cavern of her arms. Cori immediately released her, relaxing.

"No, of course not!" she declared, knowing she had to shake off this depression for Dolly's sake. "I'm going to go clean up, put on something pretty, and then—I don't know—how would you like to go to a movie or something?"

She thought that over, then wrinkled her button nose and gave her head an almost imperceptible shake. "I'm kind of too tired," she said.

Cori straightened and repositioned herself, noting again the pale face, the dark circles. She laid a hand across Dolly's forehead. It was cool and dry, but she wasn't particularly reassured.

"Are you feeling well?"

Dolly sighed. "My nose is stuffy," she said, "but mostly I'm just tired."

"Hmm. Well, I think you'd best get to bed then, don't you? We'll have a steamy bath and put on our clean jammies and slide into a cool bed. How does that sound?"

"Fine."

"Would you like me to fix you a snack while you're soaking?"

"Naw. I'm not hungry."

"You didn't eat much dinner."

Again those little shoulders shrugged. "I wasn't hungry then, either."

Corinne rubbed her niece's chin. "You'll feel better after a good night's sleep," she said, but she made a mental note to keep a close eye on the child.

This might simply be Dolly's reaction to her own malaise and depression, but Cori had no intention of leaving anything to chance. Dolly was, after all, the single most important person in her life. Cori hugged her once more for good measure, then eased her out of the chair. Together they went out of the room and up the stairs.

Cori ran hot water for a long time before readjusting the temperature and filling the tub, so that the room was clouded with steam when Dolly slid into the warm bath. Steam was good for bronchial tubes, and a little precaution made good sense.

She saw Dolly scrubbed and clean and tucked into bed, freshly clothed in a pink cotton nightgown, before running her own bath. Geneva, too, had apparently turned in early, for the door was closed to her room, and no light showed at the bottom. She poured a single glass of wine and took herself back to her bath. She soaked for the longest time, then brushed her dark hair until it gleamed like polished ebony, and finally slid into a pair of silky, dark green pajamas. She checked on Dolly, who seemed ready to slip off into a deep slumber, then took a book to the den, where she turned on the stereo.

Unfortunately, the book did not hold her interest, and the soft music, instead of relaxing her, merely deepened her melancholy. She was about to turn out the lights and go to bed when the red light on the intercom began to blink.

She froze, her mind racing. Someone was coming into the house! She didn't know what to do. Her eyes went mechanically to the telephone beside the chair, but before she could decide to call the police, she physically reached up and smacked the speech button, demanding, "Who's there?"

Several seconds ticked by, during which her heart rate shot to Mach 1. Then, suddenly, she heard a squeak, followed by a familiar voice saying, "Cori? Is that you?"

Her eyes went wide, her mouth parting. Instantly incensed and greatly relieved, she pushed the speech button again.

"Jer-ry?"

"Ah. Found you in the den. Be right down."

She couldn't believe it. It *was* him. What was he doing here? Despite the fact that this was his home, he wasn't supposed to be here! She hardly had time to wonder before he was trotting down the stairs. She folded her arms protectively, and he burst into the room, all white teeth and fine, long-fingered hands.

"Darling," he said, reaching for her.

"Don't you 'darling' me," she shot back, neatly evading his reach. "You nearly scared me to death just now! What are you doing here?"

He smiled at her disarmingly. "I kept thinking about you spending all your evenings alone..." he began, breaking off when she rolled her eyes.

"Don't start with me!" she said. "I'm in a nasty mood as it is."

He duplicated her folded-arm stance. "I take it," he said, "that you're still on the outs with *my* boss." She glared at him mutely, too stunned to speak. He relaxed his posture with a wave of his hand. "You do recall leaving a message with my little *casa*-keeper, don't you? Well, you were busy when I phoned back, so Mother took the call."

Cori blanched, remembering the circumstances of the morning she'd phoned him—and that ringing phone later in the day while Reese was there.

Jerry raised his brows at her reaction. "Ah, the sun rises."

She lifted a hand to her forehead but didn't bother to wonder what Geneva had heard or what she might have told her son. She felt certain she was about to find out, anyway. "At the risk of repeating myself," she said, "what are you doing here?"

He slanted a strange look at her, then slowly removed his suit jacket, folded it and dropped it over the arm of the chair. While he did this, she took a moment to look him over. He needed a haircut, and his suit could use a good pressing. Apparently his "*casa*-keeper" did a mean shoe polish, however, and his shirt was a dazzling white. He'd probably shaved on the plane, because the square, classical line of his jaw looked entirely too clean. The word *pristine* came to mind. He leaned against the chair, crossed his legs at the ankle and folded his arms.

"I'll tell you what I'm doing here," he said with weighty dignity. "I'm trying to save some portion of my life!"

It made no sense to her. She brought her hands to her hips. "What are you talking about?"

"You," he said evenly, "and *Reese Compton*."

Apparently Geneva had heard everything. Well, it didn't really matter, did it? Geneva could not be held responsible, after all. Besides, Cori couldn't be sure how much Geneva had understood of what she'd heard—and neither could Jerry.

"Don't worry," she told him flippantly, correctly identifying his main concern, "I didn't let your cat out of the bag. As far as Reese knows, we were—are—legitimately engaged."

He relaxed visibly. "Cori, I know what you're thinking, but there's a lot at stake here. You know I'm being considered for the London chair. I can't take a chance on mucking that up. I have to know you're going to keep up your end of things."

"When have I not kept up my end of things?" she demanded.

"I don't know," he said, sticking his chin out. "When did you start fighting with my boss?" She felt a sense of dread at that, but glared at him, daring him to say more. He did. "I think I'm entitled to an explanation. Mother has a way of confusing things, so I'm asking you. What's been going on between you and Reese?"

"None of your business."

"Oh, yes, it is," he told her flatly. "Maybe it was dumb of me to trick you into the phony engagement, but I didn't know how else to go about it—rekindling the old fire from a distance, I mean."

"Did you really think that was going to work?"

He shrugged. "It had definite possibilities. I thought you might get to like the role, and I could be fairly certain you wouldn't be accepting any casual dinner dates with Reese looking on from next door. It just didn't occur to me that my career could really be in jeopardy over this. Until you started fighting with the boss."

She just looked at him. So the boss was supposed to be his safeguard against another man, was he? Well, it just went to prove how a person could outsmart himself. The whole thing was lamentably funny, pathetically so, but she didn't mean to laugh. She really didn't. It didn't help, though, when he bristled. That aristocratic mien suffered miserably with the addition of an expression of self-righteous pique. He looked as though he'd just caught a whiff of a particularly pungent skunk—and discovered the skunk was him.

She put her hand over her mouth, but the laughter sputtered out. At least she had sense enough to brace for the explosion. She heard a sound behind her, a little scrape of some sort, but ignored it. Right now, nothing was as important as this. The time had come, and she knew, even while the smile still lingered on her lips that this discussion was going to get nasty. So be it. In fact, she was beginning to relish the idea of a good argument. Her smile broadened as he began to rant.

Dolly dropped onto the step and listened from the relative safety of the darkened stairwell, trying to get a look at who was doing all the yelling. She'd been awakened by a scratchy male voice calling out from the speaker, the inner-*something* thing. She'd forgotten what Aunt Cori called it, but she knew it meant someone had come to the house. It wasn't Reese, because the voice wasn't all drawly and deep, but who else could it be? She wasn't worried, but the more she'd thought about it, the more she'd figured she ought to tell Aunt Cori; so she'd slipped out of bed and stuck her feet into her house shoes. She'd rubbed her eyes, shambling from the room, and yawned. Her nose was stuffed up again, and when she'd swallowed, she'd found her chest was a little tight, but she was hearing voices from somewhere, and that had claimed all her attention.

She'd continued on down the hall, pausing when she saw the light go on behind Geneva's door. The house was very quiet, despite the low murmur of voices, and she'd bitten her lip, wondering if the best thing to do might not be to go back to bed; but that was when she'd heard the laughter. That had seemed kind of weird, because Aunt Cori had been so sad lately, but Dolly had been glad to hear her laughing and had wondered again who the visitor was. Curiosity spurred her forward, and she'd made her way down the hall to the top of the stairs, and that was when she'd heard him yelling—yelling at her Aunt Cori who hardly ever did anything to make anybody yell.

She scrunched down real low and slid down another step.

"You've got some nerve!" Cori was shouting.

"Oh, God forbid I should be concerned about my job!" the man shouted back. Cori turned and strode away from the door, and that was when she saw him. Jerry. He was supposed to be a long way off. That's why they were staying here with Geneva, because Jerry was a long way off. She didn't like the idea of him being back, but she most especially didn't like the idea of him yelling at her Aunt Cori. Daddy Pope had yelled at her mother, and he'd even hit her sometimes, too, and at those times she'd always been ordered away, so she knew better than to interfere, but she had to do something.

Silently, she rose and climbed the half-dozen or so stairs between her and the top. In the hallway, she stood trembling, hearing the shouts from down below, and suddenly she wanted to cry. It was so unfair of him to get mad at Aunt Cori like that. Aunt Cori was the best person in the whole world. But how was she going to make him stop? Who could she tell?

She looked at the line of yellow light under Geneva's door, but instantly rejected that idea. Jerry was Geneva's son, and besides Geneva could already hear the fighting and wasn't doing anything about it. Maybe she was scared of him. The idea heightened her own fright, and she searched frantically for a solution. Mrs. Campbell had gone for the evening. That left Reese.

Quickly she ran into the living room, past the long couch nobody ever sat on and into the entry hall, her house shoes flapping awkwardly against the soles of her feet. She saw the lumps beside the door that were Jerry's bags and stuff, but her concern was for the dead bolt, the one she couldn't reach well enough to turn by herself. To her relief, the door wasn't locked at all.

She turned the handle and stepped out into the orange glow of the porch light. It was really dark outside and quiet, and she hated these stairs. She was always scared she'd fall. But she had to get Reese. Reese was the one they always went to when they had a problem. Reese would know what to do. She gritted her teeth and started down, her gown flapping around her legs.

It was cold. She hadn't realized it was cold outside at night. The breeze whipped around her, and once when she was going a little bit too fast, she even thought it was going to knock her over and she'd fall down the rest of the way. She caught her breath, and it hurt when the cold air went in. It hurt more when it wouldn't come back out, and when that happened she knew she was in trouble, but that was all the more reason to get to Reese. Reese would know what to do. She hit the ground, running.

She was almost through the trees when she got dizzy and had to take a moment to rest, but her breathing didn't get any better, and she knew it wasn't going to. She panicked, gasping for fresh air. She needed her medicine. She needed Cori and Reese.

Reese. She stumbled forward, lost her shoe, and went on. She kept stumbling, and somehow she got there. She put her whole hand over the little lighted button and with the other reached for the shiny knocker. It seemed like a very long time before she turned her back into the corner and slid down onto the step. She could hear him coming and knew it was going to be all right. Reese was here, and it was going to be all right. When he opened the door and she toppled over onto the floor, she actually smiled.

Reese stared at the crumpled pink nightgown wrapped about the little body at his feet. The first thing he noticed was that her shoe was missing. The second thing was the panic in her wide, wet eyes and the flush of blue around her mouth.

Not again! Then, *where the hell was Cori?*

He stepped over her and looked from side to side, but he was alone with her. Desperately, he went down on his haunches beside her. He rebelled at the sight of her. *I won't go through this again.*

But what was he to do? She needed help. She needed him. There wasn't time to rationalize. With a groan he scooped her up, relieved to see that she was still conscious, petrified she was going to go limp any moment.

"Listen to me, baby," he said calmly. "It's going to be all right. I promise. Now, we've got to get you back to the house. Do you know where the inhaler is?" She nodded, wheezing with the effort. He straightened with her, horrified by how light she felt in his arms, and carried her straight for the trees, oblivious of his bare feet and chest.

"Damn that Cori!" he muttered frantically. "Where the hell is she?"

Dolly began to sob, gasp and jerk rigidly. He mentally cursed himself and tried to calm her, ignoring whatever it was that stabbed into his foot. "It's all right, baby. It's all right. We'll find the medicine and give it to you. Everything will be fine. I promise. Just hang on, honey. Almost there. Don't you go out on me. Keep those eyes open. Hang in there, baby. Hang in."

But was it all right? Was Cori all right? He couldn't imagine what would have kept her from being there for Dolly. What if something had happened to her? What if Dolly had no one but him? He kept walking—running practically—until he got to the base of those god-awful stairs. He set his teeth and started up, silently cursing everyone who'd ever had anything to do with the construction of the damned things. But that wasn't important now. All that mattered was Dolly—and Cori. God help him.

"Where—" he panted, pumping his legs "—is the inhaler?"

She lifted a hand and pointed toward the house. He clutched her tight and kept climbing. Nothing was going to stop him now—nothing; not fear, not memories, and certainly not a flight of steps! By the time he reached the top, he was as winded as she was, but the difference was that he could breathe on his own. She couldn't.

The door was standing partly open. He sucked air and bumped it with his shoulder. Just inside he stumbled over something and almost went sprawling, but he didn't have time to worry about what it was.

"Which way, babe? Point the way."

She pointed him into the living room and then into the hallway. Before he got there he heard Cori yelling. The words rang out surprisingly clear.

"Because I love him, you idiot!"

He nearly lost it right there, and so did Dolly. She bolted upright and tried to get down. He grabbed at her, surprised at how strong she was.

"Great!" a deeper voice exclaimed. "You're telling me you're in love with Reese Compton?"

That voice belonged to Jerry Arnold. For an instant, Reese froze. What was going on here? He looked at Dolly, who had stopped struggling. She was blue around the mouth but still. He looked down the stairwell. Cori was down there telling Jerry Arnold that she was in love with him—Reese—and Jerry had the nerve to sound amused! He considered going down to welcome Jerry home with a smack in the nose, and in that moment knew what an idiot he was. He had told that woman goodbye. He had refused to feel responsible for this child. As if he could stop caring. As if he could make himself stop caring.

"Have they been fighting?" he asked, and Dolly nodded violently, her green eyes bulging. "I'll take care of it," he said flatly. "I promise."

He tossed Dolly over his shoulder, understanding now what had sent her to him. He wondered how long they'd been going at each other down there and where the hell Geneva was. Dolly wheezed and gasped, struggling against him, and he understood for the first time that she was truly frightened for Cori.

"I won't let anything happen to her," he promised. "But first I've got to take care of you. Where's the medicine?" She flung an arm in the general direction of her bedroom, considerably calmer. Emotional stress seemed to play a part in this, he noticed. He'd have to keep that in mind from now on.

A door opened on his left, and he caught the white face and white hair of Geneva Arnold. He kept going, even though he was beginning to believe this attack wasn't so bad as the last one. Dolly had lots of fight in her, just like her aunt. God, how he loved them both!

Geneva was on his heels when he entered the softly lit bedroom.

"Where the hell is that inhaler?" he barked, and the older woman scurried to the bedside table, yanking open the drawer.

He laid Dolly on the bed, very much relieved, well in control, and took the contraption from Geneva. He turned it over in his hand. "How do we do this, honey? This end go in the mouth? Then we press here, right? How many times? Once? Twice? We'll do it twice. Ready?"

She struggled up on her elbows, mouth parting. He was surprised and pleased by how calm she seemed. He put the thing in her mouth. She seemed to steel herself. He pressed the top. She gasped. He pressed again. She gasped again. That was all.

He turned a panicked gaze on Geneva. "Is that it?"

She bit her pale, creased lip and wrung her hands, drawing near the bed. "How are you, little darling? All better?"

Dolly nodded and squeaked, "Better."

Fresh relief washed through Reese. He put a hand to the top of his head and let out his own breath. "You scared the living daylights out of me," he told her. "But I guess we took care of it, didn't we?"

She nodded and took a deep, shuddering breath. "He..." She gulped. "Yelling at her!"

How she loved her Aunt Cori, and how he, Reese, loved her. He should have known there would be no way to escape this kind of love, but somehow he didn't want to escape anymore. No, indeed. Somehow he was ready to take this love in hand.

"Don't worry," he said. "He's not going to yell at her anymore." He placed a kiss in the center of her forehead. "Sure you're okay now?"

She wiped her nose, nodding, and lifted her arms about his neck. He swallowed a big, doughy lump in his throat and squeezed her carefully before settling her once more onto the narrow bed.

"Listen," he said, "there's no problem you, Cori and I can't fix. Remember that. Now, you rest. I don't want anything to happen to you. I love you, you know."

She nodded solemnly and squeaked, "I love you, too."

He grinned at her. "Funny how that happens sometimes, isn't it?" She grinned at him. Her color was already coming back. He kissed her again and got up off the edge of the bed. "Stay with her," he told Geneva. "Any problems, you come and get me."

Geneva sank onto the spot he'd just vacated, her eyes large with worry. "Jerry's a good boy," she told him shakily. "It's just that he was engaged to her."

"Yeah. Well, don't worry. He'll get over it." Geneva looked so forlorn sitting there, so fragile, and suddenly he felt a fresh compassion for her. "Jerry's going to be fine," he assured her. "I know what's really important to Jerry. I've always known. He'll get what he wants most. And so will I."

Geneva smiled weakly and nodded. Reese looked at Dolly and winked. She was just a little girl with a health problem, a *manageable* health problem, from the looks of it; but somehow she'd gotten to be his little girl. He didn't know how that had happened. He didn't care. She was the bravest, strongest, most wonderful little girl in the world, and he was going to see to it that nothing else bad ever happened to her. And she knew it, too. Somehow or other she knew it.

He thought of Kenny then, and all the love he'd felt for that little boy came flooding out of him and pouring over Dolly. Kenny was dead. Dolly needed him. Mentally he let go of one and latched on to the other. He knew that was the way it was supposed to be.

He walked out of the room and down the hallway, wondering what he was going to say. But it didn't matter. He'd think of something. He felt so good now that the immediate crisis was past. He decided he'd better get used to it, and the idea made him smile.

It occurred to him how totally ludicrous this was, strolling around Jerry Arnold's house in his jeans and bare feet like he owned the place. But it was more ludicrous to think of Jerry and Corinne together the way Jerry had apparently imagined. It just didn't work. Wrong combination. And he knew the right one.

He turned the corner and started down the stairs.

Jerry was a darned good engineer. One of the best. And he was a near genius at management. In fact, Reese would have to send old Jer to London; there just wasn't anyone else for the job, and what an amazing stroke of luck that had turned out to be!

He realized he was hearing silence from the room below, and set his shoulders grimly. Nothing to be worried about. Right was right. Hadn't he always said so? And she loved him. Oh, yes, she loved him.

He practically danced into the room and glanced around. Cori was standing in front of her computer, her arms folded, her eyes glued to his face. He liked the pajamas, especially the color. He'd like them even better lying on the bedroom floor. The very idea made him grin. He turned to Jerry. That sucker was tall. He'd forgotten how tall. And his teeth were so very straight and white.

"Hello, Jer," he said, wondering if the other man didn't feel overdressed in his rumpled suit.

"R-R-R-Reese!"

But he was looking at Cori again. She was incredibly beautiful, even with her mouth hanging open. He said the first thing that came to mind. "Everything's okay."

She blinked at him. He took another stab at it. "Dolly heard the shouting and came after me. I think the stress was a little much for her. She was in pretty bad shape by the time she got there." That got through.

"Oh, my God!"

"But she's okay now," he went on. "Honestly. I took care of it. Now I'm going to take care of this. Listen." He struck a nonchalant pose, knowing it was ridiculous, but what the hell? Might as well just say it. He lifted both brows. "Will you marry me?"

He thought she was going to faint, but by the time he got to her she was standing straight again, both hands in her hair. "Don't worry about him. He's going to London."

She gasped, her eyes big as saucers. "You—you're serious!"

He grinned. "Naw. I've been serious too long. Now I just want to be happy." He slid his hand up her back and into her hair at the back of her neck. "I need you for that." She twisted to the side and threw both arms around him. He laughed. That felt pretty affirmative.

She squeezed him, then abruptly pushed away. "What about Dolly? Is she really all right? This is going to happen again, you know, and after what happened—"

"What happened happened," he said. "That was Ken. This is Dolly." He shrugged. "We'll get through. We have to. I realized tonight I couldn't turn my back on her. Maybe I knew it all along, but I was just too cowardly to face up to the responsibility."

She threw her arms around him again. "You're not a coward," she said. "You're wonderful!"

He knew she was crying, and he hugged her and couldn't keep from laughing. "I love you," he said, and she brought her mouth down hard on his. A throat cleared. Ah, yes. Jerry.

Reese took her head in both his hands and gently broke the kiss. She gave him one long look and slipped to his side, her arms about his waist. He cleared his own throat. "Uh, Jer, I realize this isn't exactly what you expected to come home to."

"He didn't expect to come home to me," Cori put in. "Not really."

Reese glanced down at her upturned face, surprised to find her brow creased. She pulled away a little.

"You want to explain that?" Reese asked, switching his gaze to Jerry.

Jerry made a strangled sound and ran a hand through his blond hair. "It's all my fault," he began uncertainly. "I tricked her. We weren't really engaged. I just told everyone that so—well—so she couldn't meet someone else while I was gone. I told her it was because of you, that you wouldn't understand her living here otherwise. I told her my job depended on her going along with it," he finished miserably.

"And she bought it because she didn't know any better!"

"Only at first," she confirmed. "It did make a strange sort of sense in the beginning, but then I got to know you...." She had a guilty look on her face. "I wanted to tell you, but I'd promised."

He stared at her, wondering how it might have been if he'd known. *You'd have run,* he told himself, *just like you've run from every other available woman.* So it was best this way.

He disciplined a smile. "Corinne," he said, "I understand all about promises. I've made a few myself, and I intend to keep them. I'll make you another one right now. I promise I won't ever be so dumb that I let you get away from me again. Your turn."

She beamed and pressed her face up against his. "I promise I'll be a good wife," she whispered. "And mother."

"I'm going to hold you to it, too!" He kissed her, feeling as though he'd just closed the biggest deal of his life, and no doubt he had.

But there remained yet another matter. He broke the kiss and looked at Jerry. "I don't like you very much just now," he told him flatly, "but I'm not a complete idiot. London's yours if you want it, because you're the best man for the job—and because it's damned convenient to have you away from here. It's up to you."

Jerry put together a very composed smile. "I'd be delighted."

"I bet you will, but don't think I trust you, Jerry. I never really did, and that makes me as sorry a friend as you. I guess the best way to handle it from now on is to keep it strictly business."

The taller man's chin had gone up, but he managed to swallow down any indignation. "I can live with that," he stated imperiously.

"You'll have to," Reese told him. "Now if you'll excuse us, there's a little girl waiting upstairs." He turned Cori toward the door, then stopped. "One more thing— whatever story you want to put out," he said, "we'll go along with it."

Jerry shrugged. "The engagement was broken days ago," he said. "It was ill-advised to begin with. We both realized it."

Reese nodded. "That'll do. See that you stick to it."

"Absolutely."

"So long, Jer."

They started up the stairs together. It was dark, and she put her arm through his. He wasn't wearing any shoes, and she started to giggle about that.

"What are you laughing about?" he asked, and pulled her against him.

His arms went around her, and she kissed him, too deliriously happy for words. He laughed against her mouth. She hugged him hard. Had this really happened? It all seemed so crazy: Jerry showing up; Dolly going after Reese. Poor darling!

Cori pulled away. "Where is she?"

"In her room."

"Is she really okay?"

"I think so. The attack seemed primarily emotional, but she does have a runny nose."

"We can fix that."

"I'm beginning to think we can fix nearly anything," he said, and she squeezed his hand. "Let's go."

"Where to?" she asked, climbing the stairs at his side. "After we get Dolly, I mean." They reached the top, and he stopped to push her against the wall, his hand finding the soft fullness of her breast. She gasped aloud, absolutely thrilled.

"Home," he said, his forehead against hers. "I want you close by, near to hand, so to speak."

She smiled. "What about the neighbors?" she teased, running her hand over his chest.

"What neighbors?"

"For a Puritan, you're awful brazen," she said.

"Look," he told her. "I've been running around the neighborhood half naked all night. Now I want to get our kid and go home and tuck her in and tuck *you* in."

"And?" she coaxed.

"And make wedding plans. Can I help it if I'm hopelessly old-fashioned?"

"I like old-fashioned," she said, going up on tiptoe to rub her nose against his. "And I love you. We're going to be so happy, Reese."

He grinned at her. "I know we are."

"And Dolly's going to be okay. I know she will. We're getting this allergy thing under control, and we're going to learn to live with the asthma."

He gave her a lopsided grin. "Promise?"

"Promise."

That seemed to be all he needed. He was a man of his word, Reese Compton, and he expected as much from her. She wouldn't disappoint him. Or Dolly. She seemed to remember making a promise of sorts to her earlier, something about marriage being forever and doing it right the first—only—time. Promises were important, and she meant to keep hers. Always.

They walked down the hall together, arm in arm, and in a little while, they took their Dolly home.

*   *   *   *   *

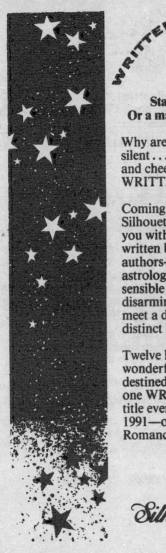

WRITTEN IN THE STARS

**Star-crossed lovers?
Or a match made in heaven?**

Why are some heroes strong and silent . . . and others charming and cheerful? The answer is WRITTEN IN THE STARS!

Coming each month in 1991, Silhouette Romance presents you with a special love story written by one of your favorite authors—highlighting the hero's astrological sign! From January's sensible Capricorn to December's disarming Sagittarius, you'll meet a dozen dazzling and distinct heroes.

Twelve heavenly heroes . . . twelve wonderful Silhouette Romances destined to delight you. Look for one WRITTEN IN THE STARS title every month throughout 1991—only from Silhouette Romance.

STAR

Silhouette Books®

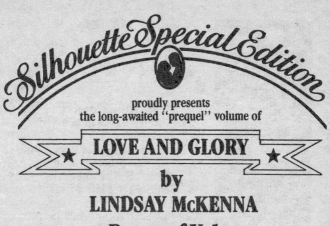

Silhouette Special Edition

proudly presents
the long-awaited "prequel" volume of

★ LOVE AND GLORY ★

by
LINDSAY McKENNA

Dawn of Valor

In the summer of '89, Silhouette Special Edition premiered three novels celebrating America's men and women in uniform: LOVE AND GLORY, by bestselling author Lindsay McKenna. Featured were the proud Trayherns, a military family as bold and patriotic as the American flag—three siblings valiantly battling the threat of dishonor, determined to triumph... in love and glory.

Now, discover the roots of the Trayhern brand of courage, as parents Chase and Rachel relive their earliest heartstopping experiences of survival and indomitable love, in

Dawn of Valor, Silhouette Special Edition #649.

This February, experience the thrill of LOVE AND GLORY—from the very beginning!

DV-1

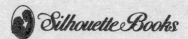

Silhouette Books

Take 4 bestselling love stories FREE

Plus get a FREE surprise gift!

Silhouette romances are now available in stores at these convenient times each month.

Silhouette Desire
Silhouette Romance

These two series will be in stores on the 4th of every month.

Silhouette Intimate Moments
Silhouette Special Edition

New titles for these series will be in stores on the 16th of every month.

We hope this new schedule is convenient for you. With only two trips each month to your local bookseller, you will always be sure not to miss any of your favorite authors!

Happy reading!

Please note there may be slight variations in on-sale dates in your area due to differences in shipping and handling.